TOM ANGLEBERGER

AMULET BOOKS
NEW YORK

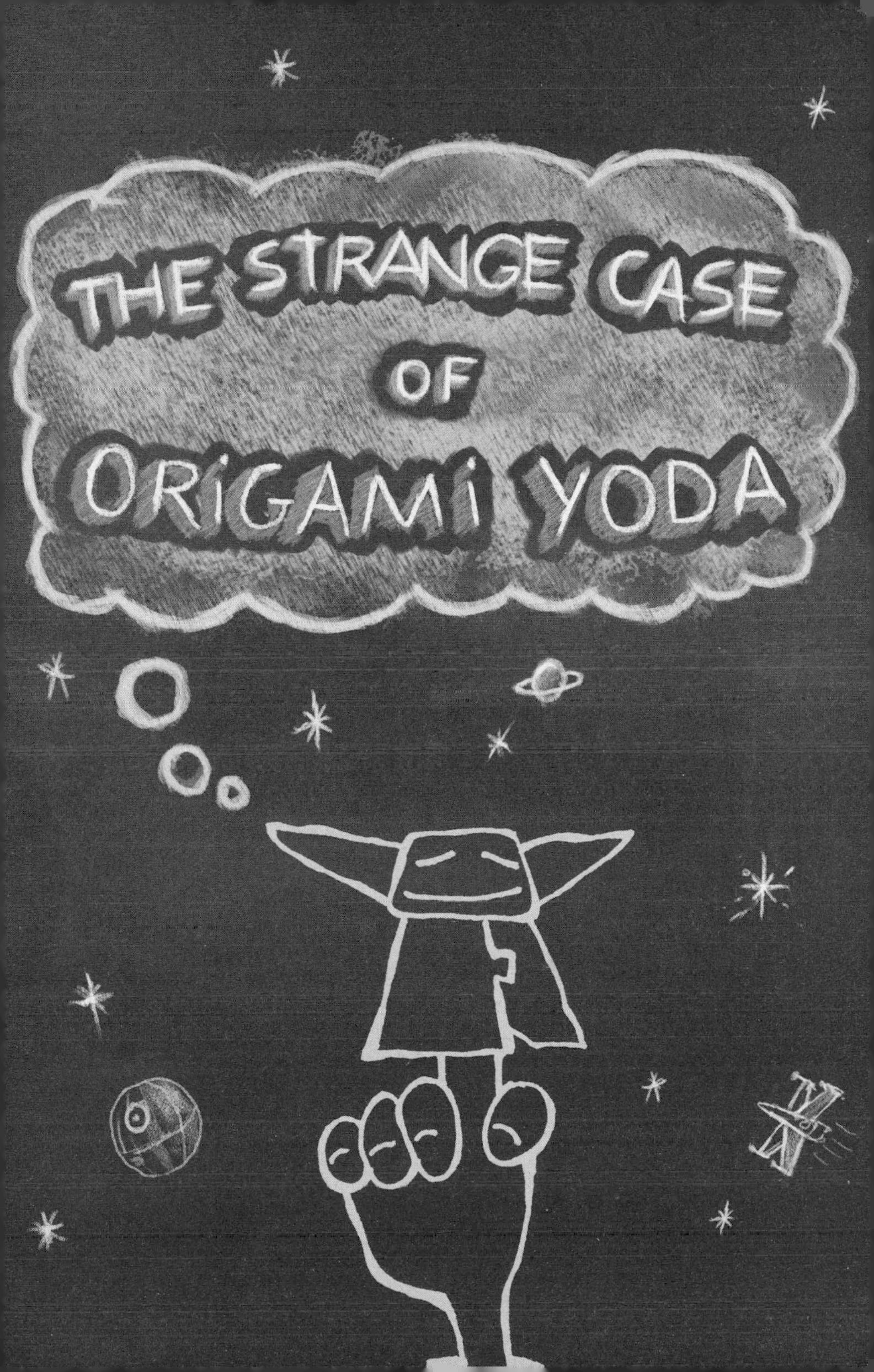
THE STRANGE CASE
OF
ORIGAMI YODA

The Library of Congress has cataloged the hardcover edition of this book as follows:

Angleberger, Tom.
The strange case of Origami Yoda / by Tom Angleberger.
p. cm.
Summary: Sixth-grader Tommy and his friends describe their interactions with a paper finger puppet of Yoda, worn by their weird classmate Dwight, as they try to figure out whether or not the puppet can really predict the future. Includes instructions for making Origami Yoda.
ISBN 978-0-8109-8425-7
[1. Yoda (Fictitious character : Lucas)–Fiction. 2. Finger puppets–Fiction. 3. Origami–Fiction. 4. Eccentrics and eccentricities–Fiction. 5. Interpersonal relations–Fiction. 6. Middle schools–Fiction. 7. Schools–Fiction.] I. Title.
PZ7.A585St 2010
[Fic]–dc22
2009039748

Paperback ISBN 978-0-8109-9650-2

Text copyright © 2010 Tom Angleberger
The cover and front matter illustrations are by Tom Angleberger and Jason Rosenstock. All other illustrations are by the author. The cover illustration and all other illustrations depicting Yoda and any and all other *Star Wars* properties are copyright © 2010 Lucasfilm Ltd. Title and character and place names protected by all applicable trademark laws. All rights reserved. Used under authorization.

Book design by Melissa Arnst

Printed and bound in U.S.A.
10 9 8 7 6 5

ABRAMS
THE ART OF BOOKS SINCE 1949
115 West 18th Street
New York, NY 10011
www.abramsbooks.com

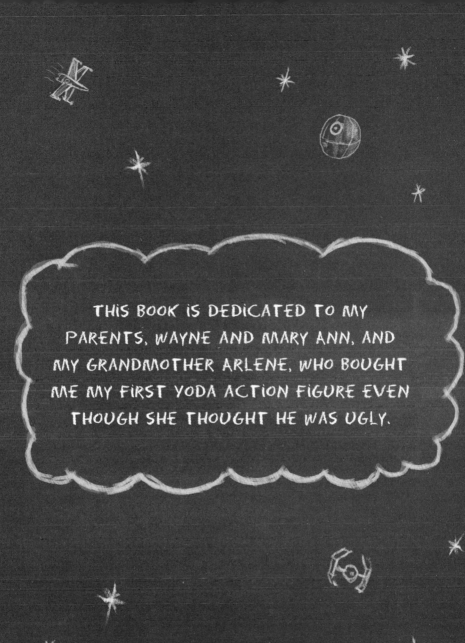

THIS BOOK IS DEDICATED TO MY
PARENTS, WAYNE AND MARY ANN, AND
MY GRANDMOTHER ARLENE, WHO BOUGHT
ME MY FIRST YODA ACTION FIGURE EVEN
THOUGH SHE THOUGHT HE WAS UGLY.

ORIGAMI YODA AND DWIGHT

BY TOMMY

The big question: Is Origami Yoda real?

Well, of course he's real. I mean, he's a real finger puppet made out of a real piece of paper.

But I mean: Is he REAL? Does he really know things? Can he see the future? Does he use the Force?

Or is he just a hoax that fooled a whole bunch of us at McQuarrie Middle School?

It's REALLY important for me to figure out if he's real. Because I've got to decide whether to take his advice or not, and if I make the wrong choice, I'm doomed! I don't want to get into all that yet, so for now let's just say it's about this really cool girl, Sara, and whether or not I should risk making a fool of myself for her.

Origami Yoda says to do it, but if he's wrong . . . total humiliation.

So I've got to know if he's real. I need solid answers. I need scientific evidence. That's why I went around and asked everybody who got help from Origami Yoda to tell their stories. Then I put all the stories together in this case file. Who knows, maybe this case file could even be useful if scientists ever decide to study Origami Yoda.

To try to make it really scientific, I let my friend Harvey comment on each story. Harvey has never, ever believed in Origami Yoda even for one second, and he still doesn't. In fact, he says he is 100 percent sure that Origami Yoda is just a "green paperwad." So he tried to find the "logical explanation" for all the really weird things that happened.

And then I commented on each story, too, because after all, I'm the one who's trying to figure this whole thing out.

My other friend Kellen wanted to help, too. So I let him borrow the case file. Instead of adding anything useful, he just doodled all over it! I was mad at first, but actually, some of the doodles almost look like people from school, so I didn't bother trying to erase them.

And anyway, I don't have time for that. I've got to study this thing and make a decision: Is Origami Yoda real, or isn't he?

Oh yeah, one other thing I almost forgot about: Dwight.

Dwight is the guy who carries Origami Yoda around on his finger.

The strangest thing about Origami Yoda is

that he is so wise even though Dwight is a total loser.

I'm not saying that as an insult. It's just a fact. Dwight never seems to do anything right. Always in trouble. Always getting harassed by other kids. Always picking his nose. Always finding a way to "ruin it for everyone," as the teachers say.

If he would just listen to Origami Yoda's wisdom, like the rest of us, he would have it made.

But no, he ends up barfing in class because he ate thirteen servings of canned peaches at lunch, or stealing a girl's shoe, or wearing shorts with his socks pulled up above his knees.

He even manages to turn his good points into loser points. See, he is the total origami master of our school. First he made cranes and frogs and all that, then he started inventing his own stuff. Origami Yoda is not just a perfect paper version of Yoda, he's also Dwight's own design.

Dwight's not the first person in the world to make an Origami Yoda, of course. There are a bunch of them on the Internet. But Dwight didn't download instructions; he actually created his own Origami Yoda.

But it's one thing to make a paper Yoda, and it's another to ask people to talk to it. That's what makes him a loser. You can't go around school with a paper Yoda on your finger talking to people.

I bet even Origami Yoda would tell him that, if he would just listen.

Anyway, here's the first story, which happens to be about a girl (not THE girl) and shows how good it can be to listen to what Origami Yoda has to say.

ORIGAMI YODA AND THE NIGHT OF FUN

BY TOMMY

It was the night of the April PTA Fun Night, the monthly dance in the school cafeteria.

Everybody comes to the PTA Fun Night. I don't know why. I don't even know why I go. I hate them. And so do a bunch of us who don't dance or flirt or do Public Displays of Affection.

The cafeteria has a stage at one end for assemblies. And if you don't want to dance, you can sort of sit on the edge of the stage.

Some people dance. Some people walk around. We sit on the edge of the stage.

There's usually me and my best friends, Kellen and Harvey. Harvey is the tall one with the smirk on his face; Kellen is the thin one who is trying to look cool by nodding his head to the music; I'm the short one with hair that's a pain in the butt to try to keep combed.

HARVEY
NOT COOL

And then there's Lance, Mike, and Quavondo. They're on the stage because most people won't talk to them. Why not? Because Lance is weird and Mike cries all the time and Quavondo is the famous Cheeto Hog. They're social outcasts. I don't know why they come to Fun Night, because they have even less of a chance of dancing with a girl than I do.

There are a few girls who sit there, too, like Cassie and Caroline. I don't know why they sit on the stage—just shy or something, I guess. I don't think they even talk to each other.

And there's Dwight, of course. I know we already look like nerds sitting on the stage

Yeeha! It's time for McQuarrie Middle School's

WILD WEST FUN NIGHT

We'll have a rootin' tootin' good time,
so get ready to boot, scoot, and boogie!!

Where: Music in the cafeteria, basketball in the gym
When: Friday, April 6 @ 7   **Cost:** $2 or 1 canned food item

like that, but Dwight somehow makes us look worse. At last month's Fun Night he suddenly decided he could dance, and he started doing this weird jumping-around thing.

Wait, it gets worse. He bumped into this popular girl, Jennifer, who was carrying a drink from the snack table, and made her spill it.

It gets worse still. Dwight goes, "I'll clean it up," and jumps on the floor and scootches around on his stomach. Then he stands up with a huge wet spot on his shirt and starts dancing again.

Believe it or not, it gets worse STILL, because he says to Jennifer, "Would you care to dance, m'lady?" After she says, "No way," he walks back over to us. With everybody watching!

"Man, you're just embarrassing us," Harvey said. "Why do you even try? Nobody's ever going to dance with you. Why can't you just play it cool?"

"You mean just stand here doing nothing like you guys do?" asked Dwight. "Okay."

And he froze right there and stood there the rest of the night without moving. He was still standing there when I left.

As far as I know, that's the only time any one of us from the stage has ever asked a girl to dance. It's not that we don't want to. In fact, we spend most of each Fun Night debating whether we should and wishing a girl would just come up and ask us instead. (One time I almost got Kellen to ask Rhondella to dance, but his mother came to pick him up right before he was about to do it.)

This time, Kellen and Harvey were trying to get me to ask Hannah, who was hanging around between the stage and the snack table.

"She's just standing there all by herself," said Kellen.

"Yeah, and I'm pretty sure she likes you," said Harvey.

I know better than to trust Harvey, but I

was kind of tempted. I mean, Hannah's not the girl I like best—that's Sara, who I am 100 percent afraid to ask to dance.

HANNAH

But Hannah's always been pretty nice to me. Maybe she would say yes. Then maybe Sara would see us dancing and get jealous and decide she wanted to dance with me, too, and then she would ask me and I wouldn't have to ask her!

After all these times of just standing there watching, just the idea of finally asking a girl to dance made me start to get all freaky—even if it wasn't Sara, it was still a girl and it would still be dancing. (Thank goodness the PTA Fun Night never has any slow dances where you touch each other!) My hands were shaking and my stomach was excited like the time my dad accidentally drove into a fire hydrant.

Yes, I thought, this is my chance. I'm going to do it.

I was actually starting to walk over to

Hannah when Dwight hopped off the stage and stopped me.

"Better ask Origami Yoda first."

"Ugh, can't you crawl back in your hole?" said Harvey. "Didn't you embarrass us all enough the last time?"

"Maybe I'm here to stop you from getting embarrassed," said Dwight. Then he held up his right hand, and there was his paper Yoda finger puppet on his finger. "Ask Origami Yoda."

Now, we had all seen Origami Yoda before, but this was the first time Dwight had asked us to talk to it. It was a historic moment, but I didn't know it then.

"Would you put that away?" hissed Harvey. "You're making us all look like losers."

"Fine," said Dwight, and he started to walk away. "I just thought Tommy needed some help."

"He needs all the help he can get," said Kellen. "What's your advice?"

"I don't have any advice," said Dwight. "But Origami Yoda does."

Then Dwight wiggled the finger puppet and made this weird, squeaky voice: "Rush in fools do."

"Is that supposed to sound like Yoda?" said Harvey. "That's the worst Yoda impression I've ever heard. Here's what Yoda sounds like . . ."

And Harvey started repeating every Yoda line from every *Star Wars* movie.

But Kellen and I ignored him and started trying to figure out the advice.

"Yoda always mixes his words up," I said, "so I bet he really meant 'Fools are in a rush.' That makes it sound like I would be a fool to rush over there and ask Hannah to dance."

"Yeah, I agree," said Mike. He and Quavondo and all the kids on the stage were listening. The whole thing was getting really embarrassing.

"Are you saying he shouldn't do it?" asked Cassie.

"I'm not saying anything," said Dwight. "Origami Yoda is."

"That is the dumbest thing I've ever heard in my life," said Harvey, who had finally stopped his Yoda impressions. "Tommy, if you miss dancing with Hannah because of Dwight's green paperwad, then you are a Super-Fool. Go do it."

"Just hold on a minute," I said. "There's no need for me to RUSH over there."

"Aw, dude, you're just looking for an excuse to be a chicken," said Kellen, pushing me. "Go ask her!"

"Give me a minute!"

Just then this seventh-grader, Mark, who is about two feet taller than me, comes in and Hannah practically runs over to grab him. And they kiss each other right there in the lunchroom, which is a Public Display of Affection and totally against the rules and furthermore disgusting to watch.

"Good thing you listened to Origami Yoda," said Dwight.

Yes, it was a good thing! It was a great thing. Can you imagine if I had been asking her to dance when that big stud guy came along? Man, she would have knocked me down to get at him and I would have been a laughingstock. Harvey would have been going wild with that big donkey laugh of his. Even Kellen would have been busting a gut.

So, basically, Origami Yoda saved my butt!

That's when I started listening to Origami Yoda, and eventually a lot of other people did, too.

Harvey's Comment

Oh yes, I believe! I believe in Paperwad Yoda! Wooo!

I believe he's a real, actual, genuine piece of paper stuck on the end of Dwight's real actual genuine finger. And I believe Dwight is the real, actual, genuine biggest nut since Mr. Peanut.

But do I believe there's something magic about Paperwad Yoda? Of course not. That's stupid.

Even the real Yoda is not real. He's a puppet in some movies and just a computer thing in others.

And even if Yoda was real, he lives "in a galaxy far, far away." I think he'd have better things to do than tell Tommy not to make a fool of himself.

Speaking of which, remember Yoda's advice: "Rush in fools do"? That's not even a Yoda quote! My stepdad told me "fools rush in" is from a song Elvis Presley sang in the 1960s.

My Comment: Okay, Dwight is weird, I already said that. But his advice was really, really good. And Yoda's not a paperwad, he's origami and he really looks like Yoda.

But I can't decide if Harvey is right or not. I mean, I don't actually believe in real magic, but Origami Yoda has done some pretty amazing things. Not long after he helped me, he saved Kellen from making a gigantic fool of himself.

ORIGAMI YODA AND THE EMBARRASSING STAIN

BY KELLEN

All right, uh, this is Kellen here . . . Uh, Tommy asked me to, uh, write down what happened with Origami Yoda, but I, like, hate to write things down. That's too much like homework, having to write a bunch of stuff down. And make complete sentences and all that. I'm like no thanks, dude. So I'm just going to record it on this . . . uh. . . . recording thing and let Tommy write it down. So . . . uh . . . I guess you can edit out where I say . . . *uhhh* . . . and stuff like that.

RECORDING THING

What happened to me was this: I was in the bathroom right before school was about to start and I saw that someone—probably Harvey—had written "Kellen Drinks Pee" on the wall over the sink, so I leaned across the sink to erase it and I had on these light brown pants and they got all wet right across the front.

It seriously looked like I had peed in my pants. Really bad. I tried to cover it with my shirt, but it was that really shrimpy shirt of mine with Scooby-Doo on it and it wasn't long enough to cover the pee part. Which wasn't really pee, of course.

Lance was in there, too.

"Dude," he said, "that doesn't even begin to hide your pee stain."

"Lance! You saw this isn't a pee stain, right? It's just water from the sink."

"Yeah, I saw that, but, man, it totally looks like you peed in your pants!"

"But you'll tell people the truth, right?"

BE FORE

"What am I supposed to do? Follow you around and tell people, 'It's not pee, it just looks EXACTLY like pee'?"

Then the warning bell rang for homeroom! That meant I had one minute to get to class.

NOT PEE

AFTER

There was no way I could get the pants dry in one minute, and there was no way I could go to class with a giant pee stain! Which really wasn't pee.

For one thing, Harvey is in my homeroom, and you know he's a total dipwad about stuff like that and he would say something loud, and everybody would see it, even people who don't normally look at me. Even worse, Rhondella is there, too, and the last thing in the world I need is for Rhondella to see me with a pee stain. Which wasn't really pee, you know.

Then I had an idea.

"Hey, Lance, will you run to class and get my coat? I think it's long enough to hide the spot."

"No time, dude, I'd never make it back

here and then back to class in one minute. Speaking of which, I got to get to class now, dude! You got about forty seconds left! See ya, Kellen."

So Lance left. Thanks, Lance.

Right now you might be thinking, so what, just show up to homeroom a little late. Great idea, except for various reasons I've shown up a little late about twenty times this year and Mr. Howell said the next time it happened, I'd have to spend the rest of the day in ISS. (That's in-school suspension and it's more boring than anything you could imagine.) Plus, every time I get sent there, Principal Rabbski sends a note home to my parents and I lose my PlayStation for two weeks.

MR. HOWELL

So I had to get the pants dry in forty seconds, except for the fact that it was physically impossible to do that.

Then Dwight came out of one of the stalls. (You know, it seems like he's in the bathroom every single time I go in there.)

"Look at my pants, Dwight. You got any ideas?"

"I'm getting the idea that you peed in your pants."

"No, I didn't. And I meant do you have any ideas that would help me?"

"No," he said, and then he held up Origami Yoda, which was on his finger. "But Yoda might."

"Whatever," I said.

Then Dwight did his Yoda voice, which Harvey is right about being totally the worst Yoda impression of all time. I do it a lot better.

But anyway, Yoda said:

"All of pants you must wet."

"What?"

"I guess," said Dwight in his normal voice, "he means you need to make all of your pants wet so it doesn't look like a pee stain anymore."

Then he left for class, too.

I turned on the water and splashed myself

all over. My pants and my shirt, too.

Then I ran to class and got there just before Mr. Howell was shutting the door.

"Should I even ask why you're all wet, Kellen?" asked Mr. Howell.

"Nope," I said, and sat down real quick. He was skeptical, but he went ahead and took roll. After homeroom, I had P.E., so I was able to switch to my sweatpants for the rest of the day.

Everybody wondered why I was wet, and sure, it was cold and uncomfortable for a while, but the important thing is that I didn't get sent to the office, I didn't lose my PlayStation for two weeks, and nobody—including Rhondella—thought I had peed in my pants!

That's when I knew that Origami Yoda is for real, man! He's totally Jedi wise!

AFTER
AFTER

WISE→

Harvey's Comment

What a bunch of malarkey. If Paperwad Yoda was real—which it isn't—surely it could come up with something better than going to class in soaking-wet pants. The real Yoda would have dried them with his mind or something.

Also, I have to point out that according to Kellen's story, Dwight walked out of a bathroom stall with Paperwad Yoda on his finger. That's just gross, folks!

My Comment: I agree that the solution was not perfect, but it's better than anything I can think of. Remember that Kellen only had a few seconds left. I think it was pretty good advice, and probably better than anything Dwight would have come up with.

That's what really blows my mind. Dwight can barely function! He walks around school with his shoes untied and his hair uncombed. He is always getting terrible grades and getting sent to the office for being late or falling asleep in class or whatever. And he DOES come to class with weird stains on his clothes.

If you asked his advice, it would be terrible. But if you ask him for Yoda's advice, you get something great. That's how come I think Origami Yoda might be for real.

For instance, this next story is about softball. The two worst softball players in our P.E. class—and maybe in the whole world—are Dwight and Mike. So how come Yoda/Dwight was able to give Mike such great advice?

EVER NOTICE HOW MUCH MR. HOWELL LOOKS LIKE JABBA THE HUTT?

MIKE

ORIGAMI YODA AND THE HOME RUN

BY MIKE

Origami Yoda changed my life!!!!

I mean, how long has it been that playing softball in P.E. has been driving me insane? It's been a long time. A looooooong time. Since we started playing Wiffle ball in first grade.

All I've ever wanted was just to hit the doggone ball, man. But it was always strikeout, strikeout, strikeout, with the occasional little bloop that would go straight to the jerk pitcher, who would throw it to the jerk at first base for an easy out.

I may as well admit how I would cry afterward, because everybody in school already knows that anyway. But there's a difference between "boo-hoo" tears and the tears I get, which are because I'm so angry. At least, I think there's a difference. Nobody else seems to think so.

BOO-HOO TEAR

I just kept thinking that if I could get a hit, maybe even a home run, I would be a hero and everyone would forget about the strikeouts and the crying, but here's what happens instead:

"This will be the one," I say to myself. "I'll show them, I'll blast it down their throats!"

ANGRY TEAR

And then I swing and miss. Then I swing and miss again and get even madder. Then I look out and see how they're all just waiting for me to strike out. They're so sure they know every freaking thing about softball! At this point I know that I'm so angry that if I hit the ball, I will knock it a mile. Then I miss a third time, and that's when I get so angry that I cry.

That wasn't that big a deal in the first grade, but it is now. A really big deal. Everybody knows me as the kid who cries during P.E. And that's not good.

So then I saw Dwight's Yoda puppet save Tommy at the dance. Well, Dwight's a nut, but I figured maybe he had tapped into the Force or something. (I totally believe in the Force and have spent a lot of time trying to focus my mind so that I can tap into it, too.)

So one day at lunch I went over to where Dwight was sitting with Tommy and those guys and said, "Yoda, can you tell me how to use the Force to hit a home run?"

"You wish home run to hit why?" asked Yoda.

"Well, I mean, I want to win, right? That's why you play a game, isn't it?"

Yoda didn't say anything, but he was looking at me with his two tiny little eyes.

"I mean, I want to be a hero for once, right?" I said. "I'm tired of always striking out."

Yoda still just looked at me.

"I mean, they hardly even pay attention when

I get my turn. And they all think they're so great because they hit the ball or because they can catch it when it comes to them. They're always shouting stuff at me, bossing me around. I'm sick of it."

Yoda still just looked at me.

I looked around at Tommy and Kellen and the others.

"I mean, you guys feel the same way, right? You're tired of Tater Tot and those other jocks always winning, too, right? I'd love to show them they aren't better than me."

"Better than you they are," said Yoda.

Everybody started laughing.

"Hey, shut up!" I shouted. "You're a jerk, Dwight! All of you!"

And I left. Man, I was really mad. Tears were starting!

But then I realized Dwight had followed me back to my table.

"Yoda's not finished, Mike," said Dwight.

"Leave me alone," I said. The last thing I

needed was for everybody to look over here and see me crying again.

But Yoda spoke anyway. "Let go of your feelings, Mike. Hate and revenge to the dark side only lead."

Then Dwight walked away.

So when it was time for P.E., I was stuck in my usual position with no help from Origami Yoda at all. (Or, at least, it seemed that way.)

I'm always last, so I didn't get up to bat until near the end of the second inning. It's crazy, because as much as I hate softball and hate to bat, I also can't wait until it's my turn.

So I stood there with the bat and suddenly remembered what Yoda said about letting go of my feelings. Maybe he was a little right about that, I figured.

Maybe if I could clear my brain of thinking about how much I hated softball, Tater Tot, the pitcher, the whole other team, and Miss Toner,

FEEL THE FORCE, MIKE!

then the dark side of the Force would go away and the good side of the Force would help me hit the ball the same way it helped Luke blow up the Death Star.

The ball whizzed past me; I didn't even have time to swing.

"Strike one," said Miss Toner, our P.E. teacher, who is the umpire.

I tried not to be mad. Even if I had swung, I probably would have missed and gotten a strike anyway.

Another ball went by. "Ball one," said Miss Toner.

Nothing to be mad about there. That's the first time I've ever gotten a ball. Normally I always swing at everything because I'm so worked up.

The next pitch was way too high. I usually swing at those. This time I just stood there. "Ball two." Maybe I'll get walked, I thought.

So I let the next pitch go by, too. "Strike two."

That wasn't working. I knew I needed to try to actually hit the ball.

When the next pitch came, a tiny voice in my head seemed to say, "Swing." Was it Yoda's voice? So I swung. "Strike three," said Miss Toner. "Good try, Mike."

I walked back to the bench trying to figure out what had happened. Had I misunderstood Yoda? Was Dwight just full of crap? Was his Yoda puppet just some kind of pointless joke?

I went up to Dwight and said, "Well?"

And Yoda said, "Cry you did not."

He was right. I hadn't cried. I hadn't even thrown the batting helmet on the ground. I hadn't made a fool of myself, for once.

Just then, Tater Tot came up to bat and smashed the ball a long, long way. Another home run.

Yes, I realized, Yoda was right. Guys like Tater Tot really are better than me. At softball, that is. So why hate him? And why cry about it?

Since that day, I'm still striking out mostly, but I also get walked some, too. But none of that really matters. The important thing is I'm not crying about it or even getting mad about it. And now that I'm spending less of my time hating people like Tater Tot, I think I'm getting closer to using the Force myself. At least I'm not going to the dark side anymore.

Harvey's Comment

Uh, I thought Mike asked Paperwad Yoda to help him hit a home run. If all he wanted to do was walk a few times, I could have told him how to do that. Most of these kids can't pitch at all, so if you just stand there and wait, you'll get walked. It doesn't take Yoda to figure that out.

I am glad Mike stopped crying, though, because that was getting old.

My Comment: As usual, Harvey totally missed the point. Yoda's point was that there are more important things than home runs. Which is good news to me, because I've never hit one, either.

SARA

ORIGAMI YODA AND THE TWIST

BY SARA

Rhondella and Amy and I sit at one table in the library every morning before school, and Kellen and Tommy and all those guys sit at the next table. They are noisy and annoying and spend half their time blabbing at us.

We've talked about moving tables, but we haven't, and I think it may be because Rhondella doesn't mind Kellen trying to flirt with her as much as she says she does. And Amy and Lance often end up talking about science fiction and stuff. I may have my own reason for staying, too, but that's my business.

If nothing else, it gives us something to laugh about—usually Harvey.

YEE HA!

So this one time, the guys were fussing at Dwight about Origami Yoda. Dwight was loving it. He loves to play dumb, but he's got this sly smirk on his face. He's my nextdoor neighbor, so I've been seeing that sly smirk for about ten years.

Have I told you before about the holes he digs in his backyard? Just digs them and then sits in them and then fills them back up. He may not be dumb, but he is definitely weird.

The first time we saw him at school with the Yoda finger puppet, Rhondella and Amy were like, "That's so weird," and I was like, "Not compared to sitting in holes all day."

Anyway, Dwight was totally digging all the attention he and Yoda were getting.

"I can't help it," he was saying. "If that's what Origami Yoda says, then that's what he says."

"But it doesn't make any sense," groaned Kellen. "I asked him where I lost my jacket, and he's like, 'The Twist you must learn.' "

"That's all he's saying to anybody," said Tommy. "I tried to ask him something, too, and so did Lance. At

first I thought it was really the answer to my question, but he keeps on saying it. I think he's lost it."

"He never had it," said Harvey.

They kept yammering like that for a while, and we tried to ignore them. Then Dwight gets up and comes over to our table with Yoda on his finger and says, "The Twist you must learn."

Then he goes over to the next table, and the next, and pretty soon he has told everybody in the library to learn the Twist. Then he left the library, apparently to spread Yoda's "wisdom" to the rest of the school. Like I said, after ten years I've gotten used to it.

"So, what is the Twist?" I asked Tommy.

"I don't have any idea," he said.

"Why don't you Google it?" asked Amy.

All the computers were taken, but Lance was using one, so Tommy and Kellen went over to ask him to look it up.

"Too bad they didn't ask me," said Harvey. "I know all about it."

Big surprise. Harvey thinks he knows everything.

"'The Twist' was a song on the *Spider-Man Three* soundtrack," he said.

"Wait a minute," said Rhondella, "you bought the *Spider-Man* soundtrack?"

"*Spider-Man Three*. Of course. I have the ones from the other two, too."

We looked at each other and tried not to giggle.

"Don't you remember that part in the movie when . . ."

We tuned him out. Kellen and Tommy came back and told us it was some old song, and Harvey goes, "We already know that!" and acted like an idiot as usual and then the bell rang. Maybe we do need to move to another table or another room . . . or another school.

That night Amy was over at my house for supper and so was my grandmother. My grandmother is at our house all the time now that she and my granddad got divorced.

AMY

Amy and I were looking up stuff on YouTube and we couldn't think of anything else to look up. Then Amy said, "Why don't you look up 'the Twist'?"

"You really think it's on here?" I asked, but I was already typing it in.

There were tons of Twist videos, it turned out. We picked one and a guy comes on like from a real old TV

show and says, "Come on, baby, let's do the Twist!"
Then they start playing this song—real old-timey but
not bad, I guess.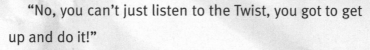

That's when my grandmother pops in.

"Are you two doing the Twist up here?"

"We're listening to it."

"No, you can't just listen to the Twist, you got to get
up and do it!"

And she sort of squatted down and started wiggling
her knees back and forth and waving her hands.

I wasn't too embarrassed. I've gotten used to her
doing strange stuff in front of my friends. But then she
starts singing along but changing the words, "Come on,
little Sara! And her friend Amy." It didn't even match the
song. She kept on singing and insisting that we try it, too.

So we did, and it turned out to be fun. Once you start
swinging your knees and your arms to the beat, it's
pretty easy.

We had just started getting into it when it was time
for supper, but my grandmother wanted to keep
dancing. My parents were going out that night, so after
supper I called Rhondella to come over, and she and

DANCE GRAMMY DANCE!

Amy and my grandmother and I did all kinds of crazy dances that Grammy used to do when she was a kid, and we had a great time and, seriously, I haven't seen my grandmother that happy in a long time. Not since the divorce and not before it, either.

I don't know how Dwight—or Origami Yoda—could have known it would work out like that, but it did and it was awesome.

Harvey's Comment

Excuse me while I get a tissue. A tear is rolling slowly down my cheek after reading that. It's like a Hallmark Channel movie. It's so bee-yoo-tee-ful.

My Comment: Well, maybe it really IS beautiful. It does sound like a lot of fun. However, I wish Origami Yoda had just told Sara about the Twist and not everybody else, because I wasted half an hour in my room practicing it by myself.

harvey

THE ARGUMENT ABOUT DWIGHT

BY TOMMY

This part isn't really about Origami Yoda giving advice. It's about an argument Kellen and Harvey and I had about Dwight.

I wouldn't bother putting it in the case file, except that to figure out Origami Yoda, I've also got to figure out Dwight. And I've got to figure out if Dwight is trying to trick me for being a jerk to him sometimes. And this is about a time when I guess I really was a pretty big jerk.

One day at lunch, Lance comes over and sits in Dwight's seat at our table. Now, that

LANCE

wouldn't be a big deal, but we didn't have any extra seats, so Dwight would have to go somewhere else.

"Dude, I hate to be a butt, but that's Dwight's seat," I told Lance.

"No, it's not," said Harvey. "It's Lance's seat now. Nobody ever asked Dwight to sit here. He just sits here. But I asked Lance to sit here, so that overrules Dwight."

"Where's Dwight going to sit?" asked Kellen.

"Hopefully on the other side of the cafeteria. Or even better, on the other side of the planet."

"Dude," said Kellen, "he's not that bad."

"Yes, he is," said Harvey. "He is a giant goober."

"We can't all be perfect like you," Kellen told him.

"I may not be perfect, but I'm not half as annoying as Dwight," said Harvey.

"Yeah, you're twice as annoying," said Kellen.

That's when we saw Dwight come out of the lunch line with his tray. He is always near the end because he sort of wanders around instead of run-walking to the cafeteria like everybody else.

"Here he comes," said Kellen. "Lance, you better go."

"NO!" said Harvey. "Let's vote. I vote Lance. Kellen votes Dwight. Tommy, how do you vote?"

"Well," I said, wishing I hadn't been dragged into it, "maybe Lance should stay."

"No thanks," said Lance. "You guys are all annoying."

He got up and left and Dwight sat down and started poking holes in his hamburger with a straw. I couldn't tell if he was acting weird because he overheard me or because he always acts weird. Just thinking that maybe he had overheard was enough to make me feel kind of barfy for the rest of the day.

RESULT OF POKING HOLES IN A HAMBURGER WITH A STRAW! NOW, SQUEEZE IT OUT + EAT IT!

BLAH HA HA

ALL ABOUT DWIGHT

BY TOMMY, WITH HELP FROM HARVEY

Why did I vote to dump Dwight? Well, Harvey does have a point about him. In fact, he has a lot of points. Believe it or not, walking around with a paper puppet on his finger all day is not the weirdest thing Dwight does. Not by far. Here are the Top 10. (These may also be evidence about whether Dwight is just making up the whole Origami Yoda thing or not.)

10. Back in the third grade, for my eighth birthday, my mom made

juice and cupcakes for the whole class. Before anybody gets a cupcake, Dwight takes a big mouthful of juice and someone makes a joke (which wasn't even funny) and Dwight spews the juice all over the cupcakes. So, no cupcakes.

9. He lies down on the floor in weird places. Like, you'll be looking for a book in the library and there he is lying in front of the encyclopedias.

8. One day, Miss Toner sent him to the equipment locker to get a dodgeball for P.E. He never comes back. So Miss Toner sent Lance to go get him. Dwight was in the equipment locker beating on the door and shouting, "Squirrels! Come save me!"

Lance opened the door for him

and Dwight goes, "Oh, I thought it opened the other way."

7. Last year, in the fifth grade, he wore the same T-shirt to school for an entire month because he got it for free from some place. It said: "Biggie Size Your Combo for Just 39 Cents!"

6. He makes a knuckle-popping sound that makes a lot of people want to barf. It also happens at the strangest times, like once when I was giving an oral book report on *Dear Mr. Henshaw*. The pops are so massively loud that I think he's faking them. I'd love to know how he does it. He just puts his hands up to his chin and all of a sudden: *KRAK!*

5. Sometimes when we decide to be nice to him, he acts like a jerk and just says, "Tycho Brahe has

a wax nose," or something weird like that.

4. Last year, he tried to get people to call him "Captain Dwight."

PRINCIPAL RABBSKI

3. "Captain Dwight" wore a cape until Principal Rabbski made him stop.

2. When he's not actively annoying us, he's usually sitting there like a hypnotized chicken, staring into space and completely ignoring everybody.

1. One time a Native American came to school to tell us about his traditions. Then he asked if there were any questions. Dwight asked, "What did you wear for underwear before Columbus brought regular underwear?"

And here's the biggest mystery about Dwight: You can never decide if he does these things to be funny or if he's just totally nuts.

Nobody ever laughs WITH him, so how can he think he's funny? But if he's totally nuts, then how come he can have a normal conversation some days or fold origami or get straight A's in math (but nothing else)?

The next story is about one of those times when Dwight actually seemed pretty smart, though still very, very weird.

HOW DID DWIGHT THINK WE WERE GOING TO OPEN THE DOOR ANYWAY?

I LIKE NUTS!

CASSIE

ORIGAMI YODA AND SHAKESPEARE'S HEAD

BY CASSIE

The reason I asked Origami Yoda a question was because I broke Mr. Snider's Shakespeare head.

I don't know why Mr. Snider wanted to have a statue of Shakespeare's head in his classroom to begin with. For one thing, it's ugly, and for another thing, I don't think we've read anything by Shakespeare. If we did, I wasn't paying attention.

Another thing I don't understand is how there can be all these stupid, clumsy, loudmouth boys in our class—like Harvey and Kellen—who are always flopping around and throwing stuff and acting like idiots, but none of them ever knocked over the Shakespeare head. And then I come along and the thing practically falls over on its own when I walk past.

But anyway, that's how it is. I was the one who broke it. It fell off the windowsill, hit the floor, and busted open like one of those hollow chocolate Easter bunnies. I think the fact that it was hollow probably means it wasn't a real statue, but I was still scared to death when I broke it.

I wasn't sure exactly what the punishment for breaking Shakespeare's head was going to be, but I figured it would be pretty big.

Luckily, I was the only one in the room right then. Mr. Snider was in the teachers' lounge, and most of the other kids were in the library, where they hang out every day before school. I tried to do that, but if you don't have anybody in particular to hang out with, there's nothing to do. And I don't have anybody in particular. I just started school here in January and I haven't found anybody I like to hang around with yet.

Anyway, Shakespeare's head was in about six

pieces. I took all the books out of my backpack, then I scooped up Shakespeare's pieces and stuffed him in there.

Then there was nothing to do but wait and see what would happen.

I sat there through the whole class with Shakespeare's head in my backpack, and nothing happened.

Then, just before class was over, Mr. Snider noticed that Shakespeare's head was missing.

"What happened to Shakespeare?" he asked. I just sat there.

"Did you guys hide him somewhere?" he asked. I just sat there.

The bell rang. I started to head for the door.

"Whoa, hold up a second. Sit back down," said Mr. Snider. "It's okay if someone's playing a joke, but I expect to see Shakespeare back here tomorrow. He has sentimental value to me. So make sure he's back tomorrow. All right?"

I just sat there and so did everybody else. I was afraid Mr. Snider was going to look at me, but he was mostly looking at Dwight, who I guess was the most likely suspect since he's weird enough to actually want a Shakespeare head.

"All right, go on," he said at last, and we all jumped up and left.

So far, so good. I was out the door with the Shakespeare pieces in my backpack. Once I got home I could trash it and I'd be safe. I felt bad for messing up Mr. Snider's "sentimental value" or whatever, but what could I do about it?

At the end of the day, I got on the bus with Shakespeare still in my backpack. Dwight got on and sat down next to me. He sits with me every day. Or actually, I guess I sit with him. When I started riding the bus in January, the only seat nobody was saving for somebody else was next to him. Usually he's talking about robots or spiders or something, but today he started right away asking about my backpack.

"To be in the backpack or not to be in the backpack, that is the question," he said in sort of a British accent or something.

"What?" I said. The word "backpack" made me jump. Did he know?

"Shakespeare, Shakespeare, wherefore art thou, Shakespeare? The backpack, perchance?" he said.

"Shhhhh!" I whispered. "How did you know?"

"Elementary, my dear Cassie," he whispered back, but with the same weird accent. "When we rode the bus to school this morning, your books were in your backpack. But now I see that you are holding your books on your lap, yet your backpack is quite full. Therefore, something else must be in the backpack. It's obvious what it is."

"Are you going to tell Mr. Snider?"

"No need," he said. "I saw him watching you and your enormous backpack when you left class. He's probably testing you to see if you bring it back or not."

"But I can't bring it back," I whispered. "It's broken!"

"Dear me, what a calamity," he said. (Still in the weird accent, by the way.) "May I see the victim?"

I unzipped the backpack a little so he could peek in.

"By George, it looks like murder, all right. What did you use? The lead pipe or the candlestick?"

BUS # 3263827

"No, it was just an accident!"

"If it was an accident, why did you sneak the victim out of the room?"

"I didn't want to get into trouble."

"Ah, but now you're in much more trouble," he said. "As the Romans said, '*Vorpius de liporius octo*': The cover-up is worse than the crime."

Well, now I was really worried, and I have to admit that I was starting to cry. If I didn't bring it back, Mr. Snider would think I had stolen it. If I did bring it back, he would know I had broken it and might even think I had done it on purpose. Either way, he would know I tried to get away with it.

"What should I do?" I asked.

"Maybe you should ask Origami Yoda," said Dwight.

"I'm serious!" I said.

"Origami Yoda is serious, too," said Dwight.

"Forget it," I said.

The bus was still about ten minutes from my house, and after I sat there for five minutes without thinking of anything, I finally asked Yoda.

"All right," I said, "what does Yoda think I should do?"

Dwight put Origami Yoda on his finger and said, "New one must you make."

"What's he talking about?" I said. "I can't make a new one."

"He said you 'must.'"

"But I can't."

"You must."

"But—"

"MUST!" shouted Yoda.

I was glad when my stop came.

By the time I walked up our driveway, I was thinking that Dwight was crazy and Origami Yoda was crazy, but that they were probably right.

I knew I couldn't make a new one that would fool Mr. Snider, but maybe I could make one good enough to replace the broken one so that he would know I didn't kill Shakespeare on purpose.

And that's exactly what happened.

I called Mom at work and asked her to stop by the Dollar Corral and get me about ten dollars' worth

MORE REALLY PLAY-DOH DO NOT EAT OR LICK!

of that fake Play-Doh they sell. I told her it was for a school project, which was true.

I used the broken parts of the old Shakespeare as a guide and I did a pretty good job, although the fake Play-Doh was bright blue and red, so Shakespeare ended up being red with a blue wig.

When I showed it to Mr. Snider the next morning, he laughed his head off and wasn't mad.

He said that the new Shakespeare would have even more sentimental value than the old one. And it's still sitting there in his classroom, although it's gotten really dry and crumbly and sometimes the nose falls off. But you can stick it back on if you lick it first.

Harvey's Comment

Was that supposed to be Shakespeare? I thought it was Robert E. Lee's horse.

My Comment: One of my main theories is that Origami Yoda must be real, because Dwight is too clueless to think of the smart things that Yoda says. But Cassie's story makes me wonder about that, since it shows that Dwight can think on his own without Yoda's help.

But the next story suggests the opposite: Not only is Dwight not wise enough to be Origami Yoda, he's not smart enough to listen to Origami Yoda. Of course, this time around neither was I.

NOSE →

ORIGAMI YODA VS. THE VAMPYRE

BY LANCE

Everybody was going to this movie called *Parasite Within: Legend of Vampyre*. But my parents won't let me go see R-rated movies. But everybody was going! But if you say that to my parents, they make some kind of sarcastic remark about jumping off a bridge, which makes no sense.

I asked Yoda what to do, and Dwight makes this croaky voice and says: "Stinks movie does."

So then I said to Dwight, "But I thought you were dying to see it."

"I am," Dwight said. "It's gonna be awesome!"

And then a second later he switches to his Yoda voice and waves the paper Yoda and says, "Down two thumbs are. Cheesy are the effects special. Money save you will."

So I ended up not going—not that I had any choice, because of my parents.

On Monday I asked everybody how it was and they all said it stunk and that the special effects were cheesy and they had wasted their money! Even Dwight.

Harvey's Comment

Big whoop. The logical explanation for this one is so simple: Dwight had read a review of the movie online or something. Or maybe he just guessed that a movie with a stupid title like that would be a stupid movie.

My Comment: Man, I wish I had listened to Origami Yoda. That movie was SO LAME!

MARCIE

ORIGAMI YODA AND THE NASTY EIGHTH-GRADER

BY MARCIE (EIGHTH GRADE)

Origami Yoda is the dumbest thing of all time! He's a total fraud! If you think he's anything more than a piece of paper, you're an idiot.

I know this because I believed in him and ended up looking like an idiot.

It's my own fault for listening to a bunch of sixth-graders!

One of the kids on my bus is the dipwad who walks around with the Yoda on his finger.

One day all these sixth-graders kept saying, "Ask Origami Yoda anything! He knows everything!"

And they told some stories about how Origami Yoda had predicted some stuff. Well, it sounds stupid now, but they all seemed to believe it, and I did have a question I wanted answered.

See, I won my homeroom spelling bee and I was about to compete in the school-wide spelling bee. And if you win that, you get to go to the county spelling bee, then the regionals, and if you win that, you get to go to Washington, D.C., for the national spelling bee, which will be on TV! And you can win prizes, too. Like this eighth-grader last year made it to the regional spelling bee and won a hundred-dollar savings bond.

I wanted to win, obviously, but studying these stupid little booklets of words you've never heard of is BORING!

And it's impossible to memorize words when everybody's talking about Origami Yoda and asking him questions about stupid junk.

So I said, "Origami Yoda, can you tell me what word I need to learn to win the spelling bee?" (Man, I feel like such a fool for talking to a finger puppet now that I know it's just a finger puppet, but remember, everybody told me it was magic. Yeah, right.)

The kid held Yoda up so I could see him and he made this stupid voice and said, "Tomorrow tell you I will. Rest now I must. Far into the future must I look."

And the kid put Origami Yoda away and wouldn't get him back out.

"Thanks for nothing, fartface," I said. "Now will you people shut up so I can learn my words?"

Well, the next day when I got on the bus, the kid immediately holds up Yoda and says, "Mulked."

"What?"

"*Mulked* learn to spell you must. Forget not the *T*."

"Okay, so how do you spell it?"

"Look it up," said the kid. Twerp!

But I did look in the little booklet and it was actually in there. Only it wasn't spelled *mulked*, it was spelled *mulct*. That's exactly the kind of rip-off word that nobody's ever heard of that they love to use in spelling bees.

Well, seeing it in the booklet convinced me. I fell for it like a total sucker. I was sure that word would make me the school champ. I didn't bother with the booklet anymore.

Finally, it was time for the spelling bee, which was

held in the cafeteria with the whole school watching. All my friends and everybody in my homeroom was cheering for me.

The thing about spelling bees is the first round is always a freebie. I had to spell *brown*. Nobody went out on the first round.

Then I had words like *without*, *frankly*, and *politics*.

Then in the fifth round I got the word *vestidge*. At least, I thought it was *vestidge*. It turned out to be *vestige*. The judge rang a little bell and I had to sit down and watch the rest of the spelling bee like everybody else. I was furious.

This little sixth-grader won it by spelling *muscular*. That's right, *muscular*, not *mulct*! Nobody ever got *mulct*! I was even more furious!

After school, on the bus, I told the Yoda kid what an idiot he was, and I told everybody that Origami Yoda was a worthless piece of paper.

But like I said, I'm the real idiot for believing in something that stupid anyway.

Harvey's Comment

Finally! I'm glad someone else has seen through this nonsense. Although, frankly, I'm surprised an eighth-grader would fall for it in the first place. (By the way, I came in second in the school spelling bee and would have won if the judge had pronounced the words better.)

My Comment: Actually, I don't think Harvey gets the point of this story, either. It's not just the fact that Origami Yoda was wrong. The question is WHY was he wrong. I wonder if he was really wrong or whether this was a Jedi Mind Trick.

Think about it:

Dwight tells Marcie that Yoda will give her an answer the next day.

Instead of saying thank you, she calls him fartface.

Now, maybe Origami Yoda could have figured out the real winning word. We'll never know.

But the question is, why would Dwight want to help a girl who had just called him fartface? Maybe it was Dwight or maybe it was Yoda, but I think one of them purposefully gave her the wrong word to make her lose!

If she had looked up "mulct" in a dictionary, like I just did, she might have figured it out. It has a couple of meanings. One is when you punish somebody. The other is when you trick them. I think Dwight and/or Origami Yoda did both.

ORIGAMI YODA AND THE CHEETO HOG

BY QUAVONDO

Origami Yoda helped me a lot, even though Dwight didn't want him to. I went up to Dwight and said, "I need Yoda's advice," and Dwight said, "Go away, Cheeto Hog."

The whole "Cheeto Hog" thing was what I needed Yoda's advice about in the first place!

What happened was, the sixth grade went on this field trip to the zoo and we saw this vending machine next to this snack bar up near the buffalo. Mr. Howell had told us we weren't allowed to get anything from the refreshment stands or the ice-cream carts. But he hadn't said anything about the vending machines.

So we all ran over to the machine, and I got there first. The bags of snacks cost two dollars each! These were tiny little bags that, like, usually cost maybe seventy-five cents at the Qwikpick.

But I had money that my mom had given me for the trip, so I shoved it in fast before somebody could push me out of the way.

Right then, as soon as my second dollar went in, Mr. Howell comes over and starts shouting at us. Basically he told us that we should have known that he meant we couldn't get stuff from vending machines, either. How was I supposed to know that?

Everybody started grumbling, but at least they hadn't lost two dollars in the machine.

"But, Mr. Howell," I said, "I already put two whole dollars in and I haven't pushed the button yet!"

"Good grief," said Mr. Howell. "Can you push the coin return button, Quavondo?"

I pushed it and nothing happened. Everybody was standing around watching all this, by the way—Harvey and Tommy and Tater Tot and just about every boy in class.

ZOO ALERT!

CAUTION: LOOSE GORILLA!

"All right," groaned Mr. Howell, "go ahead and get something, Quavondo, but that's it. Nobody else. I mean it. This is a big waste of money."

So I pushed the button for a bag of Cheetos and the bag came out and I picked it up and it felt like there was almost nothing in it. It was even smaller than the seventy-five-cent bags!

So I turn around and there's half the class wanting me to share my Cheetos. Look, I wouldn't have minded sharing with one person, but there probably weren't enough Cheetos to even give everybody one. And I was hungry!

So that's when things got nasty and people started grabbing at them and I ended up stuffing them in my mouth and then I started to choke on them and Harvey said, "Serves you right, Cheeto Hog." And everybody laughed.

And instead of stopping them, Mr. Howell just said, "That's why I didn't want people buying food." Well, if he had said that in the first place, maybe I wouldn't have wasted two dollars and practically choked to death!

So ever since then people have been real mean to me and keep calling me Cheeto Hog, and one day during math I needed to borrow an eraser and no one would lend me one until Mr. Howell forced Kellen to give me one.

I NEVER GOT IT BACK EITHER!

So, obviously, I was getting tired of all that and I had heard about how Yoda helped Mike stop being a softball crybaby, so I figured I would ask for his advice. But Dwight wouldn't let me.

"O-nay ay-way, eeto-Chay og-Hay," he said.

"C'mon, Dwight, that's what I need to ask Yoda about."

"Orget It-fay," he said.

But then something really scary happened! His right hand shot up in the air, and the Yoda puppet was on one finger.

"Cheetos for everyone you must buy," said Dwight in his Yoda voice. And then he put his hand over his OWN MOUTH! But he kept on trying to talk!

"Assembly during tomorrow will be," he mumbled through his hand. "Then the Cheetos give you must. Big bags must they be!"

"But I can't bring Cheetos to an assembly! You know the rule about no food in the gym! I'll get in huge trouble!"

"Better even!" squawked Yoda. "Trouble better is!"

At this point Dwight—still covering his mouth and still talking as Yoda—put his coat over his head and crawled under the lunch table.

Everybody was looking, of course.

"But I can't do that," I said to Tommy and Kellen, who were sitting right there, and they said, "Shut up, Cheeto Hog!"

Well, that night my older brother gave me a ride down Route 24 to the Food Lion in Vinton.

There was no way I was going to buy a bag of Cheetos for everybody in the school. But I found out that there are 116 kids in the sixth grade, and that sounded possible.

At Food Lion, they had twelve-packs of three-ounce Cheetos bags for $5.99. So I bought ten of these packs to get 120 bags. That cost $59.90 plus tax, which was $3.58. So the whole thing cost me $63.48!

Luckily, I had fifty dollars my grandmother had sent me for my birthday, and the rest I borrowed from my brother.

The next morning, I crammed most of the Cheetos

bags into my backpack and an old Elmo backpack I used
to use. I had to leave all my books at home. And then I put
on my winter coat and stuck the rest of the bags into all
the different pockets. It was still a little chilly outside,
so I didn't look too crazy, I hope.

As soon as I got to school, I crammed it all in my
locker.

Yoda had been right about there being an assembly.
It was Mr. Good Clean Fun. Mr. Good Clean Fun comes
to our school every couple of months to talk about how
we should wash our hands after using the bathroom and
take baths and things like that. His puppet is a singing
monkey.

Mr. Good Clean Fun does his show for one grade at a
time, and us sixth-graders weren't having our assembly
until 1:30, the beginning of seventh period.

Now, remember that everybody had heard Dwight/
Yoda the day before at lunch, so everybody knew what I
was doing. And they asked me about it all day long.

"You really brought the Cheetos, Quavondo? I don't
believe it," said Tater Tot. It was working already! He
called me by my name and not Cheeto Hog!

Mr. Good Clean Fun

and **SOAPY** the monkey

present:

"Feeling good about our smells"

"Yeah, shhh, don't tell Miss Toner."

"No problem. Give 'em here."

"No, I have to wait until the assembly."

"Why?" he asked.

"Yoda said so," I said.

"Oh, yeah," he said.

I promised everybody that they would get their Cheetos.

I wasn't sure how I was going to give them out, because I knew any of the teachers, especially Mr. Howell or Miss Toner, would stop me if they saw me with them.

So I asked Origami Yoda.

He told me, "Speed must you have."

Dwight told me that I could give him his bag of Cheetos right then, but I told him what I told everybody else: "Yoda said to wait."

So when the bell rang at the end of sixth period, I just jumped up and ran without waiting to be dismissed.

Some of the other kids in the class started running after me, and when kids from other classes saw us running through the hall, they started running, too, so they wouldn't miss out on the Cheetos.

Unfortunately, Mr. Howell saw us when we ran by his classroom.

"We don't run to assembly!" he shouted.

I had secretly left my locker unlocked, so all I had to do was grab the backpacks and my coat and keep running.

Some of the boys tried to grab them, but I shouted, "No, Yoda said to wait for the assembly!"

We burst into the gym and then the feeding frenzy started. I tried to hand out the bags one at a time, but the kids just started pushing and grabbing so much I gave up.

"Just one!" I had to keep shouting. "There's one bag for everybody."

At one point I looked up and saw that Mr. Good Clean Fun was standing on the stage with his monkey just staring at us.

By the time Mr. Howell got there, everybody had a bag and was pigging out.

"What the heck is going on here! Quavondo, did you do this? What is the deal with you and Cheetos? All right, you go to the office and I'll be down later to discuss this with Principal Rabbski and write up your in-school suspension slip."

Miss Toner got there next and she blew her whistle and shouted, "The rest of you, go throw those bags away. I mean it. And don't try stuffing the whole bag in your shirt, Harvey, I can see it! I want those bags in the trash NOW!"

So I spent the rest of the day in the office. Principal Rabbski told me that I had embarrassed the school and insulted Mr. Good Clean Fun. She wrote a note that I had to take home to get signed by my parents and I had to write a five-page report about nutrition and a letter of apology to Mr. Good Clean Fun. I heard later that most of the Cheetos did get thrown away, so that was sixty-three bucks' worth of Cheetos wasted.

SORRY? YOU BETTER BE SORRY, PUNK!

But it was all worth it, because almost nobody ever calls me Cheeto Hog anymore!

Harvey's Comment

As far as I can see, all this story proves is that Dwight is crazy as a bald gorilla. I was there when he was doing that covering-his-mouth thing, and it was totally embarrassing. Why does he have to sit at our table? Why wouldn't they let me kick him out?

Anyway, Dwight's advice had nothing to do with Yoda. He just wanted to get a free bag of Cheetos. Which he got. I saw him eat the whole bag in about one second while Miss Toner was asking us to throw them away. If I had a giant mouth like he does, I wouldn't have had to try to hide them in my shirt.

Second, I have a message for Quavondo: Once a Cheeto Hog, always a Cheeto Hog.

My Comment: Harvey's all wrong. This was Yoda's best piece of advice yet. Quavondo went from being a hated Cheeto Hog to being a hero. The fact that he got in trouble for trying to give away Cheetos made everybody like him even more. And Yoda predicted that, too.

MAN, I WANTED SOME OF THOSE @!⚡☾✪* CHEETOS!!!

ORIGAMI CHEWBACCA?

ORIGAMI CHEWBACCA AND THE UNSIGNED SUSPENSION SLIPS

BY TOMMY

I've asked Dwight many times to write a chapter for this case file. He refuses to do it.

But one day when I asked, he said, "You should put these in," and he pulled a bunch of papers out of his backpack. Most of them were just crumpled up, but one had been folded into what I think was an Origami Chewbacca. Either that or a gorilla with a tie on. It wasn't nearly as good as Origami Yoda.

When I uncrumpled and unfolded the papers, I discovered that they were notes that were sent home to be signed by his parents, which had never been signed.

In-School Suspension Slip

Student: Dwight Tharp   Time: 8:36 a.m.
Teacher: Mr. Howell   Date: March 20

Reason for I.S.S.:
[ ] Combative behavior   [ ] Inappropriate attire
[ ] Tardy   [ ] Inappropriate language
[X] Other (If other, please explain): Refusal to remove finger puppet during Pledge of Allegiance.

Parent's signature: _____
Must be signed by parent/guardian and returned within two (2) school days.

In-School Suspension Slip

Student: Dwight Tharp

Teacher: Mr. Howell

Time: 10:06 a.m.

Date: April 4

Reason for I.S.S.:

[ ] Combative behavior

[ ] Tardy   [ ] Inappropriate attire

[X] Other (If other, please explain): Student was asked to work math problem on board. Ate chalk instead.

[ ] Inappropriate language

Parent's signature: _____

Must be signed by parent/guardian and returned within two (2) school days.

Student: _____

Teacher: Mr. Howell

Reason for I.S.S.:

[ ] Combative behavior   [ ] Inappropriate attire

[ ] Tardy   [ ] Inappropriate language

[X] Other (If other, please explain): Refusal to remove finger puppet during Standards of Learning testing.

Parent's signature: _____

Must be signed by parent/guardian and returned within two (2) school days.

In-School Suspension

Student: Dwight Tharp

Teacher: Mr. Howell

Time: _:_0 a.m.

Date: April 19

Reason for I.S.S.:

[ ] Combative behavior   [ ] Inappropriate attire

[ ] Tardy   [ ] Inappropriate language

[X] Other (If other, please explain): Failure to return any of previous In-School Suspension Slips with parent's signature.

Parent's signature: _____

Must be signed by parent/guardian and returned within two (2) school days.

CAROLINE

DWIGHT AND THE FIGHT

BY TOMMY

This story is weird for a lot of reasons.

First of all, it should be Caroline who tells it, but for some reason she refuses to talk to me about Origami Yoda or Dwight.

Second of all, Origami Yoda doesn't really do much, but he is the whole reason for the story. (That will make sense after you've read it.)

The other thing that's weird is that I almost got beat up trying to find out what happened!

Here's how it all started.

This girl Caroline came over at lunch.

Now, you know that I like Sara and Kellen likes Rhondella, but no one can deny that Caroline is amazingly cute and cool, too. But other than sitting on the stage near her during every Fun Night, I don't really know her, since she's in seventh grade.

She is kind of famous at school because she's a lip reader. She wears hearing aids, but I've heard that she can tell what you're saying just by watching your mouth move. I guess she must be deaf, but I've never seen her use sign language, and she seems to talk all right, although she doesn't say much during Fun Night.

Anyway, she came over at lunch one day to talk to Origami Yoda. It looked like she had been upset, maybe even crying, but now she was just mad.

"Do you have Origami Yoda today?"

"Uh-huh," said Dwight with his mouth full

NORMAL
LIPS

DWIGHT
LIPS

of food. (It's bad enough that he talks to other people with food in his mouth, but this poor girl had to try to read his lips while meat chunks were dribbling out.) He pulled Origami Yoda out of his pocket and put it on his finger.

"Well, can Yoda help me do anything about Zack Martin? Look what he did to these pencils my grandma gave me."

She held up three pencils, all snapped in half, which used to have her name on them but her name had gotten snapped in two, like this: "Caro line Broome" or "Caroli ne Broome."

"Why did he do that?" I asked.

"He just wanted to show off that he could snap pencils one-handed, so he grabbed them off my desk and snapped them all at once. I just got them last night. I hadn't even sharpened them!"

I had tried this stunt once myself, with my own pencil, of course. You put your middle

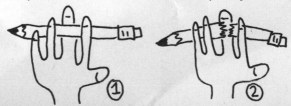

finger under the pencil and the other fingers over it, then you slap it down on a desk. In my case, the pencil just cracked a little, but my fingers hurt like crazy. Doing three at once would probably break my knuckles.

"Zack's always doing stuff like this, and I want Yoda to tell me how I can stop him."

That was a tough one, even for Origami Yoda, who sat there on Dwight's finger apparently thinking it over for a while. Then Origami Yoda whispered in Dwight's ear. Dwight actually whispered something to himself!

Finally Dwight turned to Caroline and said, "I'll take care of it."

"What?" brayed Harvey. "What are you going to do about it?"

I was thinking the same thing and I bet everyone else, including Dwight himself, was, too.

Dwight looked down to the other end of the cafeteria, where Zack was eating by himself. It's hard to miss Zack, since he's about two feet taller and 150 pounds heavier than anyone else in the seventh grade. In fact, he's closer to Mr. Howell's size than to ours. I think he failed two or three times and is probably about fifteen years old.

ZACK

I had trouble with him once. I had called some kid an idiot and the kid turned out to be Zack's cousin or something. So later that day Zack told me not to do it again, while squeezing the bejeezus out of my arm. Another time he punched Harvey in the back really hard. Harvey said it was for no reason, but probably Harvey had said something smart-alecky and deserved it.

Anyway, Zack is best avoided at all times.

Dwight turned back to Caroline and said, "Yeah, I'll take care of it."

"You don't have to do anything," she said. "I just thought Yoda might know some kind of magic way to get Zack to stop."

"I'll take care of it," he said again, and got up and took his tray to the trash cans.

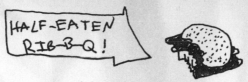
HALF-EATEN RIB-B-Q!

I'd never seen him throw away uneaten food before.

For a minute, I thought he was going to go straight over to Zack, but instead he just walked right out of the cafeteria.

When the rest of us got back to class, Dwight wasn't there. And he wasn't on the bus, either! And then he wasn't in school for the rest of the week.

But it didn't take us that long to figure out basically what happened.

When the seventh-graders were walking back to their rooms after lunch, Dwight jumped out from behind a trash can and attacked Zack.

Zack clobbered him, of course, but since everybody, including a teacher, saw that Dwight started it, Dwight was suspended for a week, while Zack only got one afternoon in ISS, even though I heard that Dwight got a big bruise under his right eye.

Various kids were able to tell me about the fight, but they hadn't heard much of what

Dwight said to Zack. When Dwight came back to school, he refused to talk about it.

When I decided to make this case file, I knew I would need to get a firsthand account of the fight, and that meant I would have to talk to Zack himself.

I borrowed Kellen's recorder and hid it in my pocket. I found Zack before school and recorded this interview:

TRANSCRIPT OF HIDDEN-RECORDER INTERVIEW WITH ZACK MARTIN

Q: I just want to ask you a couple of questions about your fight with Dwight a while back.

A: What?

Q: Look, I'm not trying to get you in trouble. I just want to hear your side of the story.

A: Whatever.

Q: Seriously, I'm not trying to get you in trouble.

A: Good.

Q: Who started the fight?

A: He did.

Q: What happened?

A: I don't know.

Q: I've talked to a few witnesses. Is it true that he jumped out from behind a trash can?

A: Yeah.

Q: Did he say, and I quote, "I know karate!"?

A: [Grunt] Maybe.

Q: Did he then attempt to kick you?

A: Right here. [Subject points to right shin.]

Q: What did you do?

A: I don't know.

Q: Did you say, and I quote, "Are you crazy?" and then push him away?

A: Probably.

Q: Is it true that he got back up and waved Origami Yoda in your face?

A: Was that Yoda?

Q: Yes, it was a Yoda finger puppet made from folded paper.

A: [Nasty laugh]

Q: Did Yoda say anything to you? Or perhaps I should say, did Dwight say anything to you in a Yoda voice?

A: That was supposed to be Yoda?

Q: Yes. Did he say anything?

A: Yeah, something crazy like, "If you knock me down, I'll get stronger."

Q: Really? Do you think it was, "If you strike me down, I shall grow stronger than you can possibly imagine"?

A: Maybe.

Q: That's from *Star Wars*, but it wasn't Yoda that said it, it was—

A: Whatever. [Subject begins to move away from interviewer/voice recorder.]

Q: Wait, can you tell me what you did next?

A: Yeah, this! [Subject puts hand on my face and pushes me into a wall.]

I decided to end the interview there.

Harvey's Comment

Well, this certainly proves that Dwight is an idiot, and if it was Paperwad Yoda's "advice" that Dwight try to fight Zack, then that proves that Paperwad Yoda is an idiot, too.

My Comment: I can't really argue with that.

I KNOW KARATE!

MANGA DWIGHT

ORIGAMI YODA AND THE SWEATER VEST

BY KELLEN

Uh, I'm going to tell this one into the recorder again, so . . .

I've got to tell this story because Tommy wasn't there that day and nobody who didn't see the sweater vest could ever describe it.

Now, normally, I would never complain about what someone else wears, because all I wear are shirts from my four-dollar-T-shirt collection and some of them are pretty stupid, which is why they only cost four dollars. But I think they're cool.

But this sweater vest was just so outrageously ugly that nobody could not notice it.

It must have been knitted by his grandmother or something, because no store would ever sell something like that.

Mostly I remember the puffballs all over it. It was barf green with a black stripe, but the puffballs were pink. Massive buttons and a big letter *D* on the front. On the back was an orange reindeer.

There's only one kid in the whole school that would ever in a million years come to school wearing that sweater vest!

And of course, that kid is Dwight!

And when one kid does something stupid, there's got to be somebody to make a huge production out of it.

And of course, that kid is Harvey.

"Man, what on earth are you wearing?" Harvey said way too loud for the library.

"Clothes," said Dwight.

"That is the ugliest thing I've ever seen," said Harvey.

"So what?" said Dwight. "Should I take it off because you don't like it?"

"Please do," said Harvey. "It's making me barf!"

"Seriously, man," I said, "you really should take it off." I was just trying to help. Maybe I was sort of laughing a tiny bit when I said it.

Dwight stomped off to another table.

Harvey never thinks he needs to apologize for anything, but I felt bad enough to go after Dwight.

"Hey, I'm sorry, dude," I said, trying to smooth things over. "But, you know, that sweater does look a little first-gradey. Did your mom make you wear it?"

"Shhh! Shut up," said Dwight, and he froze and looked straight ahead.

Caroline Broome, the broken-pencil girl, was walking into the library.

Dwight waved at her. Dwight has never waved at anybody before, except maybe imaginary squirrels or something. She waved back.

"Holy Wampa Hair! So you DO like her!" I said.

Dwight didn't say anything.

"And you wore the sweater vest for her?"

Dwight's ears turned red.

"Oh man, Dwight. Have you lost your mind? Listen, why don't you ask Origami Yoda about this stuff first?"

"No thank you," said Dwight. "Could you just shut up?"

"Let me ask him," I said. "Origami Yoda, should Dwight—"

"Why don't you shut up!" said Dwight, and he jumped up to go and grabbed his books but dropped them and a bunch of pencils.

I picked up one of the pencils. It said "Caroline Broome" on it and had a little smiley face. I think they all said that. He must have bought them to replace the broken ones.

Dwight ripped it out of my hand.

"Gimme that, JERK!" he yelled.

There's two kinds of yelling you do at school. There's the kind that's a yell but not all that loud because you really don't want to look silly or get a bunch of teachers in your face. Then there's another yell where you're so mad, you don't care about any of that stuff anymore. When Dwight yelled "JERK!" it was the second kind of yell, and everybody in the library looked up and Mrs. Calhoun, the librarian, started coming our way.

But Dwight was looking to see if Caroline was looking, and of course she was, because everyone was.

"Great! Now you've ruined everything!" said Dwight.

He stomped out of the library before the librarian got there, so I ended up having to listen to her lecture about how kids seem to think the library is some sort of playground.

Then Harvey came over and started making fun of Dwight's sweater vest some more, but I wasn't interested. And I didn't tell Harvey about Caroline and the pencils, either.

When homeroom started, Dwight wasn't wearing his sweater vest anymore. I passed him a note saying I was really sorry, and he ended up eating lunch with us later and things were sort of back to normal.

Harvey's Comment

Don't make me out to be a bad guy because I told him his sweater was ugly. I did him a favor.

My Comment: I'm just glad I wasn't there.

JENNIFER

ORIGAMI YODA AND THE BAD SINGER

BY JENNIFER (IN A TEXT MESSAGE)

I askd Yoda who ws gng 2 gt kckd off American Idol + he sed Terrell + he ws right.

Harvey's Comment

Duh! Terrell was a total loser. Everybody knew he was going to get kicked off.

My Comment: But I asked Dwight if he watches "American Idol" and he said his parents won't let him watch TV at all anymore. So how would he know anything about Terrell?

This really raises the question: Can Origami Yoda see into the future? And that's what the next story is all about, too!

TATOOINE ☆IDOL☆

ORIGAMI YODA AND THE POP QUIZ

BY SARA

Hmmm, I almost don't want to tell this story because I'm still a little bit mixed-up about it. I mean whether I did the right thing or not. But Tommy keeps asking me to tell it, so whatever.

Anyway, Amy and Rhondella and I are hanging around our usual table in the library before school, just like the last time I told you about with the Twist.

Tommy and those guys are over there talking and stuff and making a lot of noise, and I look up and see Dwight's doing his Yoda thing and his smirk thing. Same old stuff as always.

Harvey was standing over there shouting, "Man, this is so stupid," and "You guys are totally wasting your time." He is so loud! He needs like a permanent chill pill or maybe just a muzzle.

A few minutes later, Kellen comes over and talks, mostly to Rhondella, who he's clearly in love with, but to the rest of us, too.

"Guys, there's going to be a pop quiz in Stevens's class today on the parts of a leaf! Better study!"

(Mr. Stevens is the life science teacher. We have him for second period.)

"How do you know?" asked Rhondella.

"Origami Yoda told us."

"So you believe in Origami Yoda?" asked Rhondella.

"Absolutely," said Kellen. "He saved my life one time."

"How?"

"Er . . . it's kind of personal," said Kellen. "I've got to go study for the quiz."

So he left and we tried to decide what to do.

"I guess we should study," said Amy.

She and Rhondella got out their science books and

opened to the big leaf diagram, which is what we'd been studying all week.

"I don't know, guys," I said, "isn't this kind of like cheating?"

I've made it all the way to the sixth grade without ever cheating once on anything! And I didn't want to break my record for some dumb parts-of-a-leaf quiz. I knew most of them already anyway.

"What's cheating about it?" asked Rhondella.

"Well, a pop quiz is supposed to be a surprise," I said. "If you know about it ahead of time, then it's not a surprise and you're kind of cheating."

"But we don't KNOW there's going to be a test," said Amy. "All we KNOW is that one dork says another dork with a finger puppet says there's going to be a test."

"Hey, don't call Kellen a dork," said Rhondella.

"Why? Do you like him?" asked Amy.

"Ewww, of course not, but he's not a dork."

"C'mon, guys, I'm serious," I said. "Is this cheating? Because, if it is, I'm not going to do it."

"Well, unless you shut up about it, we're not going to get to do it, either, because there's only five minutes left until homeroom," said Rhondella. "So—stoma, cuticle, epidermis, chloroplasts . . ."

I really couldn't decide if it was cheating or not, so I ended up just sitting there listening to Rhondella and Amy read off the names of parts over and over.

Then the bell rang for homeroom.

MR. STEVENS

When we got to the science room for second period, guess what Mr. Stevens said.

"Take out half a sheet of paper—we're going to have a pop quiz!"

Me, Amy, Rhondella, Tommy, and Kellen all got 100s. I definitely would have forgotten the cuticle if we hadn't studied it right before class.

Harvey got an 85. Kellen said Harvey refused to study because he was so sure that Origami Yoda was wrong. And Dwight got a 60 because he didn't listen to his own puppet's advice! WEIRD!

But I felt so bad about it that I decided to go and talk to Mr. Stevens after class.

I didn't mention the names of any other kids and I didn't say anything about Origami Yoda. I just told him that I knew ahead of time that he was going to have a pop quiz.

He said there was no way I could have known that because he didn't decide to do it until AFTER class had already started! He realized he had forgotten to bring the movie he was going to show us and he needed something to fill time with, so he gave us the quiz.

So it seems to me that the Yoda puppet must be more than just a piece of paper. He was right about the Twist, and now he was right about the pop quiz.

So later I asked him a question—which is none of your business—but I think he was right about that, too!

I mean, maybe Dwight has spent so much time sitting in holes and being WEIRD that he's learned ESP or something. Or maybe Dwight's not as weird as I thought. Or maybe it's a good kind of weird. I don't know.

Harvey's Comment

If ESP existed—which it doesn't—I seriously don't think you could get it by sitting in a hole. Plus, the reason I did so bad on the pop quiz was because I had missed two days that week because I was throwing up. So Mr. Stevens let me take a retest and I got a 96.

My Comment: I kind of agree with Sara. If Yoda really is magic, then that gave us an advantage over other kids in the class.

Didn't Gandalf say, "With great power comes great responsibility"? (If it wasn't Gandalf, maybe it was Thomas Jefferson. Or Spider-Man's uncle.)

Well, this made me think that maybe we need to be more careful about how we use Origami Yoda. This next story shows how things can go wrong when using Origami Yoda.

YODA AND THE NOT-SO-SECRET SECRET

BY RHONDELLA

Kellen kept bugging me and bugging me that I had to ask Yoda a question.

"All right, fine, if it will make you shut up for ten seconds," I said.

So then he wanted me to do it right away.

Next thing I know, I was talking to Dwight, who was busy doing his stupid fake knuckle-popping sound. I know it's fake, but it still creeps me out.

"Dwight! Rhondella has a question for Origami Yoda!" said Kellen really loud, which was embarrassing.

Dwight stuck out his finger, and it had this green thing

on it. I've never seen any of those "Star Wars" movies, but I know what Yoda looks like, and this green thing looked a little bit like him, I guess.

"Question of yours is what?" Dwight screeched.

"What?" I said.

"Question of yours is what?" Dwight screeched again.

"What's his major malfunction?" I asked Kellen.

"That's what he's supposed to do. That's how Yoda talks, kind of, except I can do it better. Listen, 'Urrm, question you have, urrrm?' But anyway, you're supposed to ask him your question now."

"Whatever," I said.

"Go ahead and ask him, he's amazing," said Kellen.

Kellen and Dwight AND Yoda were all looking at me, and I realized I didn't have a question.

"C'mon," said Kellen.

So I just said, "Why is Kellen bugging me all the time?"

And Yoda said, "Likes you he does. Kissing you he wants."

And Kellen was like, "Shut up, dude!" and shoved Dwight. And then Dwight, or maybe Yoda, started yelling at Kellen.

So I just left.

Anybody could have told her that.

My Comment: Yeah, I have to agree.

In fact, the truth is that not all of Yoda's answers have been very magical. Some of them have in fact been really annoying. Sometimes the person who asked the question just goes, "DUH!" or "Whatever" and stomps off. I think we have to consider these bad answers when we try to decide if Origami Yoda is magic. For the next chapter, I've written down the ones I can remember.

KELLEN'S COMMENT:

I THINK SHE LIKES ME!

ORIGAMI YODA AND THE UNSATISFACTORY ANSWERS

BY TOMMY

Q: Origami Yoda, how do you find the grenade launcher on the Arctic Level of Operation Death Rain?

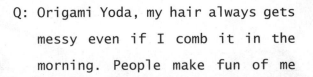

A: Read a book should you.

Q: You mean like the hint book? That costs fifteen dollars!

A: No, a book like *The Hobbit*.

Q: Origami Yoda, my hair always gets messy even if I comb it in the morning. People make fun of me

and my mom rags on me about it.
What should I do?

A: Hairdo like Yoda you must have.

Q: You mean bald?

A: Yes.

Q: Hey, Origami Yoda, have you seen
that totally hilarious YouTube
video where Chewbacca dances with
a Jawa?

A: What a Jawa is?

Q: You know, a Jawa. One of those
little guys from the first movie.

A: What this movie is?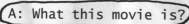

Q: *Star Wars*!

 A: What?

Q: *Episode Four*! *A New Hope*! *Star
Wars*, dude!

A: In that movie I was not.

Q: Origami Yoda, can you help me find my jacket?

A: Last place you had it remember can you?

Q: Origami Yoda, why does Dwight pick his nose so much?

A: Picks it he never does.

Q: Hah, right, that's a lie!

A: At least he eats it not, like you do.

However, to me, the most unsatisfactory answer of all time was the one I got to a VERY important question. I was afraid to ask for a long time, but I finally decided to ask Origami Yoda if Sara liked me. He seems to know who likes who, and that was information I needed bad.

HEY, TOMMY—
YOU SHOULD
TAKE THAT
HAIRCUT
ADVICE!

TATER TOT

ACTUAL
TATER TOT

NOTE:
NOT
DRAWN
TO SCALE.

ORIGAMI YODA
LETS ME DOWN

BY TOMMY

So one day I was feeling pretty pathetic about how Sara had been talking to this guy Tater Tot so much. And not talking to me at all.

There are two kinds of kids who get a name like Tater Tot: total losers and total perfect guys that all the girls love. This Tater Tot is the second kind of Tater Tot. (If I was a Tater Tot, I have a bad feeling that I would be the first kind of Tater Tot.)

I was sitting at lunch, worrying that Tater

Tot was working his Tater Totty magic on Sara.

Then I realized that it was just me and Dwight at the lunch table since everybody else had finished. Whenever we have a lunch that has gravy—like turkey or Salisbury steak—Dwight takes about five extra rolls and smears them around in the gravy. It's gross and he's always the last one done because the rest of us can't wait to get out of there.

"Hey, Dwight, if I ask Origami Yoda a question, will you promise not to tell anybody?"

"Purple."

"What?"

"Purple."

"Does that mean yes?"

"Purple."

"Okay, could you just nod yes or no?"

He nodded yes and got out Origami Yoda.

I whispered, "Origami Yoda, why doesn't Sara like me?"

"Does not says who like you she does," said Yoda (or Dwight with his bad Yoda voice, whichever).

"Wait a minute," I said, "what does that mean?"

"Purple," said Dwight.

I tried to rearrange the words:

She says who does not like you?

She does not like you. Who does says?

Who says she does not like you?

Is that what Yoda meant? Was he suggesting that I had the wrong idea? That Sara did like me?

"Does he mean Sara DOES like me?"

"Purple."

"I'm serious, man! Is that what it means?"

"Purple."

"Man, you are a pain in my butt. Let me ask Yoda another question."

"No," said Dwight, finishing his last roll and getting up to dump his tray.

"Hold on. Why not?"

"Uh, because you said I was a pain in your butt, maybe? Why should I let Origami Yoda help you if you're going to be mean? I'm sick of you guys always being mean to me except when you need to talk to Origami Yoda."

"I'm sorry, man," I said, "but if you wouldn't say stuff like 'purple' over and over and over again, maybe we would be nicer."

"I thought it was funny."

"Ask Origami Yoda if it's funny."

He asked.

"Funny it is not," said Yoda.

"See?" I said. "If you'd listen to Origami Yoda more, you would know how weird some of that stuff is. If you would just do what he says, you wouldn't seem so weird all the time."

Dwight didn't say anything. By this time we had dumped our trays and were headed to the lockers. The one-minute warning bell rang.

"So, can I ask Origami Yoda another question?" I asked.

"Brown," Dwight said, and walked off.

I ran after him yelling, "Does she like me, Yoda?"

Harvey's Comment

As far as I can tell, absolutely nothing "magical" happened here at all, except for Tommy making a fool of himself shouting "Does she like me, Yoda?" which is magically pathetic.

My Comment: Fine, I'm pathetic. At least a girl likes me. Maybe. Maybe not. As you can see, I was now super confused. It was vital that I talk to Origami Yoda as soon as possible.

THE TRAGIC DEATH OF ORIGAMI YODA

BY TOMMY

So the next day at lunch, I was still trying to get Origami Yoda to explain what he had meant about Sara.

But Dwight just kept saying, "Purple."

I was really getting mad, so I just said, "Yoda, why can't you stop Dwight from being such a loser?"

I felt bad as soon as I said it. Dwight wouldn't let me apologize.

Instead he just goes crazy!

"You want me to stop being a loser? I guess I better get rid of this, then."

And he rips Origami Yoda off his finger and balls him up.

"What are you doing?" I shouted.

"Can't be a loser anymore. Gotta be normal," said Dwight. "Better throw away this litter."

"C'mon, Dwight," said Kellen, "just relax a minute."

But Dwight went over to the trash can and threw Origami Yoda away. Then he came back and sat down again and kept eating his lunch.

"Hallelujah!" said Harvey. "Thank Jabba that's over. Now maybe you three can stop being the biggest dorks in the whole school."

"I guess that will leave you as the biggest," Kellen said.

I ran to the trash can to get Origami Yoda out. He had landed in some baked beans. I tried to wipe off the beans and uncrumple Origami Yoda and get him back into Yoda shape. But I couldn't figure out how to do it. I could sort of figure out which parts were his ears, but the rest of him had come unfolded.

OH NO! NOT BAKED BEANS!

"C'mon, Dwight," I said. "Put him back together. I'm sorry I said you were a loser."

"Purple" was all he said.

I kept trying to get Yoda back together.

Then this girl named Lisa comes over. She doesn't usually talk to us at all, but now she asks Dwight if she can ask Origami Yoda a question.

"Yoda's dead," says Dwight, and he starts crying. I mean, he was sobbing for real.

Lisa just went, "Oooookay," and walked away.

"Can't you just make a new one?" asked Kellen.

"I can't remember how," Dwight sobbed. Then he cried until lunch was over.

Harvey's Comment

→ Best. Lunch. Ever.

LISA

My Comment: Man, Harvey's comments sure are annoying. But wait, it gets worse! He demanded his own whole section! Not only is it unscientific, it's totally lies.

THE REAL ORIGAMI YODA

BY HARVEY

Geez, I don't know which was worse: Dwight blubbering about Paperwad Yoda or Tommy sitting there trying to wipe beans off of it. I've got to get some less embarrassing friends.

Anyway, the "tragic" loss of Paperwad Yoda gave me an idea. Why not make my own, real origami Yoda?

So I just went on the Web and Googled "origami Yoda." There's tons of different pages with instructions for making one.

I printed out the instructions, got some paper,

and made one that totally blows Dwight's away! It was really, really hard and I had to figure out some really tough parts, but it's like a hundred times better. I mean, it really looks like Yoda.

So I took it to school to show Tommy what a real origami Yoda looks like.

"Wow, that's amazing," Tommy said. "You must be an expert or something."

LIE ⇨ "That's a hundred times better than Dwight's Yoda," said Kellen.

"Yeah, I know it is," I said, "and it gives better advice, too."

"It gives advice? Just like Dwight's?" said Tommy.

"No, not just like Dwight's. Didn't I just tell you it gives better advice?"

"Okay, let me try," said Kellen.

"No. Try not. Do . . . or do not. There is no try," I said in a totally perfect impression of Yoda.

NO WAY! ⇨ "Wow! That's even better than my Yoda impression," said Kellen. "Okay . . . uh . . . oh, Yoda, what's my locker combination?"

"That's a stupid question," I said. "That's not advice, that's just a number. Dwight's Yoda couldn't answer that, either. Ask me something good!"

"okay," said Kellen. "Does Sara like Tommy?"

"SHUT UP, MAN!" shouted Tommy.

"oh, come on," said Kellen. "You know that's what you were going to ask Dwight's Yoda before he crumpled it."

"Will you be quiet?" said Tommy.

"Yoda has an answer for you," I said.

"All right," Tommy said, "what does he say? Does Sara like me?"

"Hates you she does," said Yoda/me. "Laughs at you with her friends she does."

You should have seen Tommy's face! Especially since right then Sara and all her friends at her table started laughing about something—probably Tommy. Right then I almost believed in origami Yoda myself.

"I'm sorry," I said to Tommy. "If I had known that was what he was going to say, I would have tried to let you down easier."

My Comment: Yeah, right. Let me down easy? Harvey thought it was hilarious.

And for the record, I never said, "You must be an expert," when I saw Harvey's Yoda. In fact, everything that me and Kellen supposedly said about his Yoda is a lie. Plus, Harvey just downloaded the instructions; Dwight actually invented his own Origami Yoda.

However, to be totally honest, I have to admit that Harvey's Yoda does look pretty good and his Yoda voice is a lot better.

I really doubted that Harvey's Yoda had any special powers, but I was afraid that Harvey was probably right. It does seem like Sara and her friends are always whispering and laughing when I'm around.

But before I could think about it anymore, something really weird happened . . .

DUEL OF THE ORIGAMI YODAS

BY TOMMY

"Wrong Harvey is," said a screechy voice. "Likes you she does. Much very."

We all turned around and there was Dwight with his own Origami Yoda!

I was triple stunned to see Yoda, to find out that Dwight was talking to us again, and to find out that his Origami Yoda thought Sara liked me.

"Where'd you get that?" Kellen asked.

"I woke up this morning and remembered how I had made the first one. I think it must have come to me in a dream."

"Good grief," said Harvey, waving his Yoda in Dwight's face. "Too bad you couldn't dream of one this good."

Dwight looked at Harvey's Yoda.

"Ah, yes, it appears you've made the Van Jahnke Yoda. One of the best Yoda folding patterns online," said Dwight. "I made one of those myself once."

"BULL-loney," said Harvey. "This one's totally better than yours."

"It's not bad at all," said Dwight, who seemed unusually sane all of a sudden, "but if you'd like some constructive criticism, try getting your creases a little crisper. That will get your corners a little neater."

GOOD CORNER

BAD CORNER

"Oh, yeah?" said Harvey. "How do you like these creases?"

And Harvey tried to crumple Dwight's Yoda.

Kellen and I stopped him. Now that Origami Yoda was back, we weren't going to let him get messed up again.

"Chill out, Harvey," said Kellen. "They're both good."

"No," said Harvey, "mine's a million times better, you guys just won't admit it."

"Find out let us," said Dwight's Yoda. "A duel of Yodas let there be."

"How are they supposed to fight a duel?" asked Harvey.

"They could both give their answers to the same question and then we can see who's right," Dwight said.

"Okay, what question?" I asked.

"We've already got the question AND the answers," said Kellen. "Harvey's Yoda says Sara hates Tommy—"

"SHHH!" I hissed. "Could you shut up, please?"

"While Dwight's Yoda says Sara likes Tommy," continued Kellen. "All we have to do is find out which one's right!"

"What do you mean?" I asked, even though I knew what he meant.

"Tommy has to go to the PTA Fun Night and ask Sara to dance. If she says yes, then Dwight wins. If she says no, then Harvey does."

"Hmmph," snorted Harvey. "I'll take that bet. For the first time ever a PTA Fun Night might actually be fun—in fact, it should be hilarious."

"Well, you can go," I said, "but I'm not."

"C'mon, Tommy," said Kellen, "you've been wondering about her all year. Why not find out? I mean, you believe Dwight's Yoda, right? Not Harvey's."

I looked at Dwight.

"Seriously now, are you sure?" I asked.

"Certain am I," said Dwight's Yoda.

"Man," said Harvey, "that is the worst Yoda impression of all time! For one thing, Yoda would have said 'Certain I am,' and for another thing—"

"Could you guys just shut up for a second and let me think?" I said.

"Sure," said Harvey. "In fact, I'll give you more than a second. But you've got to decide sooner or later, because Fun Night is this Friday."

Harvey's Comment

I've changed my mind. I do believe in origami Yoda ... MY origami Yoda!

My Comment: Yeah, right!

TRYING TO SOLVE THE STRANGE CASE OF ORIGAMI YODA

BY TOMMY

Okay, I just finished re-re-rereading the case files.

I still can't make up my mind. Some of the stories do make it sound like Origami Yoda is totally wise. But Harvey does make good points sometimes.

Oh man, it's impossible to choose. This has gotten bigger than just asking a girl to dance. Even when that girl is Sara, the girl I've been thinking about nonstop since the first day of school.

See, to not ask Sara to dance would be basically saying that Harvey's Yoda is better than Dwight's. That Harvey was right all along. I'll be choosing Harvey over Dwight.

And frankly, I've had about enough of Harvey criticizing everything and everybody all the time. Yeah, I know I've been doing that a lot, too. Like calling Dwight a weirdo and a loser. But it has gotten old. Real old.

But just because Harvey's gotten annoying doesn't mean he's not right. In fact, he probably is right. Basically all he's saying is that a really cute girl doesn't want to dance with me. That's normally a pretty safe bet.

Meanwhile, Dwight is asking me to take a huge gamble. I mean, I've kind of started to like him, but that doesn't mean I have to humiliate myself just to prove it, does it?

And why should I listen to Dwight, anyway? I mean, this is the same guy who was shouting "purple" at me a couple of days ago. The same guy who spewed on my birthday cupcakes and pops his knuckles and sits in holes AND walks around with a finger puppet.

But that takes me right back to the beginning again: Is Origami Yoda JUST a finger puppet, or is there something bigger going on here? The Force, maybe? When I read all these cases it sure seems like he's for real, but what if I'm wrong?

I want to believe in Origami Yoda. But the penalty will be so bad if he's fake.

I know I said this has gotten bigger than just asking a girl to dance, but when you get down to it, that's what it really is about and that's something I've never done.

Maybe I won't do it right. Or maybe that won't even matter because I never had a chance anyway. It will be so awful if I go up to Sara and she says no and then starts giggling with Rhondella and Amy. And then Harvey will be laughing in my face forever and ever.

It would be so much safer just to sit on the stage. But what if—

Oh man, Kellen's mom just pulled into the driveway. She's driving us over to the school for the dance. It's time to go and I haven't decided yet. What am I going to do?

WHAT HAPPENED NEXT

BY TOMMY

I just got back from the dance. It's late, but I've got to write it all down right now.

So Kellen's mom dropped us off and we went in. Kellen and I headed for the stage. Harvey was there, of course, but I didn't see the rest of the usual stage sitters. I looked out in the crowd of dancers for Sara. Yep, there she was. I had actually been hoping she wouldn't come and I could duck the whole crazy mess.

Now that I was looking at her, I didn't think I could ask.

It's one thing when Origami Yoda tells you NOT to ask a girl to dance at the PTA Fun Night, so you just sit there and don't do anything and you can see if he was right or not.

But it's another thing when Yoda says you SHOULD ask a girl to dance and you actually have to go do it. That's not so easy.

And it's even harder when there's another Origami Yoda—who admittedly sounds a lot more like Yoda—telling you that the girl hates you and laughs at you.

But it's hardest of all when you're standing there at the dance, with some kind of terrible music blaring, and a bunch of kids are jumping around in the middle of the cafeteria and you're leaning against the stage with a bunch of guys who have always been lurkers and have never asked a girl to dance and don't know how to dance and there's Sara bopping around with her friends—thank goodness not with any boys—and she's the cutest girl in the whole cafeteria by a

FAR OUT! IT'S TIME FOR MCQUARRIE MIDDLE SCHOOL'S

GET READY FOR OUT-OF-THIS-WORLD FUN!

WHERE: MUSIC IN THE CAFETERIA, BASKETBALL IN THE GYM
WHEN: FRIDAY, MAY 4 @ 7   COST: $2 OR 1 CANNED FOOD ITEM

million miles and to do this you're going to have to walk out there and ask her in front of her friends with your friends all watching from the side.

Was I really going to do all that just because a guy with a paper finger puppet said so?

I decided not to do it.

Then there was a break in the music and Sara and her friends were just standing out there talking. Maybe I would go, I thought. Then the music started again and I thought I'd better wait.

"Go do it," said Kellen.

"To your doom you go," said Harvey's Yoda, "but go you must."

I decided to stall. "Where's Dwight? I want to check with him one more time before I do it."

"I don't know where Dwight is," said Kellen, "but check out the snack bar."

We looked over at the snack bar. Lance and

Amy were standing there talking and sort of bobbing along with the music.

"And look at that!" Kellen pointed toward the center of the gym. "It's Quavondo and Cassie. Dancing!"

"The world's gone mad!" gasped Harvey.

"Look at the stage, man," said Kellen. "It's empty except for us. We're the only ones left. Even Mike is dancing."

I looked where he was pointing. "With Hannah? How did that happen? What happened to her giant boyfriend?"

Was it possible? Could Origami Yoda have changed life as we knew it?

And then came an event even stranger. An event no human could have ever predicted. The crowd of dancers sort of parted and there in the middle of it all was Dwight dancing with a girl! It was Caroline, the broken-pencil girl.

"What the heck?" said Harvey, Kellen, and I at the same moment.

As you can guess, Dwight was a terrible dancer, but that didn't seem to matter to Caroline. They were both having a great time.

"Has she gone crazy?" Harvey sneered.

But I knew she wasn't crazy. Suddenly things were starting to make sense.

"No," I said. "Don't you get it? It was Origami Yoda! This was his plan!"

"What plan?"

"Origami Yoda knew that if Dwight got beat up fighting Zack Martin in Caroline's honor that she would fall in love with him! Dwight must have taken Origami Yoda's advice for once."

"That was his advice? To get beat up by a gorilla? Great advice," said Harvey.

"But it worked," said Kellen.

Man, this was blowing my mind. Whose idea was it to have Dwight fight Zack? Yoda's or Dwight's? Or were they the same?

Then that made me think of something even more mind-blowing.

Are you ready for this?

Okay, here it is: What if this whole Yoda thing was just a hoax by Dwight to get attention? Sure, it made him look stupid at times, but as Kellen said, "IT WORKED!" Not only had he gotten attention from us and a lot of other kids who normally ignored him, he had actually gotten a girl to dance with him and maybe even be his girlfriend! That's something anyone would have said was impossible.

But if it was a hoax, then it was a totally genius hoax, and how could he have known it would work without Origami Yoda telling him it would? And, of course, if Origami Yoda did tell him, then it wasn't a hoax after all.

Now I was totally confused.

The song ended and Dwight and Caroline came over to where we were standing. They were HOLDING HANDS!

"Well?" asked Dwight. "Have you asked her yet?"

For once he wasn't acting insane or saying "purple" or being weird, but I wished he hadn't brought up that subject again. I was hoping everybody would forget about me asking Sara.

"I was thinking about waiting for the next Fun Night," I said.

Dwight let go of Caroline's hand, reached into his pocket, and pulled out Origami Yoda.

"Still do you not believe?" said Origami Yoda, shaking his little paper head sadly from side to side.

Not believe? I hated to say that I did not believe. But everything that has ever happened to me in my life involving girls suggested that Harvey's Yoda was right and that Sara was going to say no in front of everybody and everybody was going to laugh at me. Harvey would be laughing hardest and wouldn't stop for about twenty years.

Plus, if it was all a hoax, then why should I listen to Yoda at all? Maybe Dwight just wanted to laugh at me, too.

But somehow I just didn't think it was a trick. Look how many people had listened to Origami Yoda's advice and were now actually having fun at a Fun Night. Somehow having fun at a Fun Night seemed even more impossible than a magic finger puppet.

Maybe I was being stupid, but I did believe. Something was going on here that was bigger than a hoax, and I wanted to be a part of it whether it was magic or luck or the Force or whatever.

And I decided that even if Sara said no, I'd rather be on Dwight's side than Harvey's. Dwight is weird, but I guess I've started to like him, and I hated to let him down. Somehow I didn't mind letting Harvey down at all.

"I'm going to do it," I said. "Now, I mean. I'm going to ask her right now."

Harvey laughed, but Dwight gave me a big smile and it almost looked like Origami Yoda did, too.

"You're really going to do it?" Dwight asked.

"Yes," I said.

"Good, then let me tell you something, Tommy," Dwight said, and then he whispered in my ear. "Yoda didn't need the Force for this one. Yoda knows because Sara asked him about you about a week ago. She wanted to know if you liked her as much as she likes you."

"What did you tell her?" I whispered back.

"Well, Yoda told her to come to this dance and find out."

I looked up. Sara was looking at me and Dwight. She smiled at me.

Holy Jabba the Hutt! I didn't have time to think much about what all this meant as far as Yoda being real or not real. I hopped off the stage. I started walking toward Sara.

It was like a dream. Everything was perfect! It was finally going to happen!

"Just one little problem," said Harvey. "You don't know how to dance!"

I froze. He was right.

"Ha-ha, you idiot! You've spent all this time worrying about whether to ask her or not and you never even thought of what would happen if she did say yes! What a . . ."

I looked over at Dwight in desperation.

He held up Origami Yoda.

"The Force—always may it be with you."

Just then a booming voice rang out over the loudspeakers.

"Come on, everybody. Let's do the Twist."

When the song started playing, most of the kids at the dance looked around like something smelled bad. They had no idea what it was. I'm not even sure they realized it was music. They sure didn't know how to dance to it.

But we did.

Before I knew it, we were all doing the Twist. Dwight and Caroline, Cassie and Quavondo, Lance and Amy, Mike and Hannah . . . even Rhondella and Kellen. Rhondella and Kellen! Can you believe it?

And without me ever having to ask her, Sara and I were together wiggling our knees and trying to do the Twist while holding hands—which isn't easy—and laughing our heads off.

Harvey's Comment

No comment. ←

HOW TO FOLD ORIGAMI YODA

BY TOMMY

So I begged and begged Dwight to teach me how to make an Origami Yoda. When he finally showed me, I couldn't figure it out. All I could get was a blob. So Dwight taught me how to make a simpler one. You use a rectangle to start with. A half of a half sheet of paper is about right. If you can find a piece of paper that's green on one side, start with the green side down and Yoda's head and feet will be green. You have to draw his face on, but it's pretty cool and looks a lot better than the blob. Kellen drew the different steps so we wouldn't forget how to make it. Here they are . . .

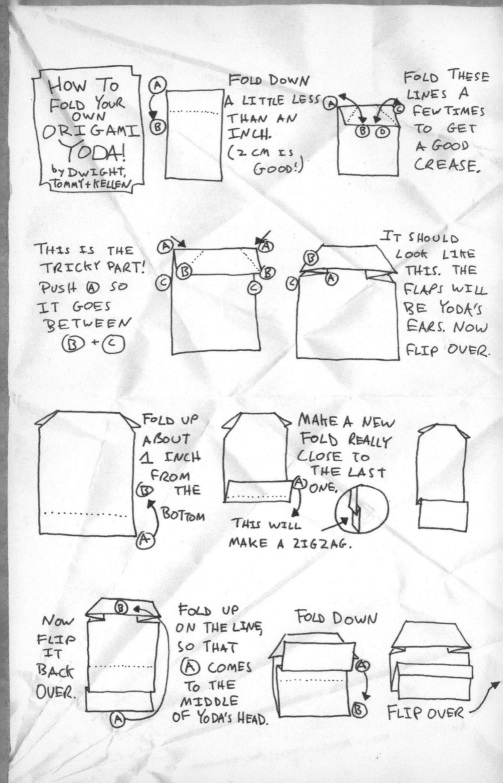

FOLD ALL LAYERS
TOWARD THE CENTER.... LIKE THIS.

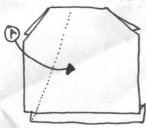

(A) REPEAT ON THIS SIDE.

DON'T WORRY IF THE
SIDES ARE A LITTLE
UNEVEN.

FOLD THE
TOP OF
THE
HEAD
DOWN.

FOLD
OUT
THE
EARS

PSSST....
A LITTLE
TAPE BACK
HERE HELPS.

FLIP OVER....

CRINKLE EARS

(IF YODA HAS ANY
EXTRA FEET, JUST
TUCK THEM OUT OF SIGHT.)

IT'S YODA!

ACKNOWLEDGMENTS

Moviemakers: George Lucas, Ralph McQuarrie, Stuart Freeborn, Wendy Midener, Nick Maley, Gary Kurtz, Irvin Kershner, Frank Oz, Lawrence Kasdan, and the many others who made the real Yoda real.

Paper folders: Akira Yoshizawa, Robert Lang, Paul Jackson, Hiro Asami, and Fumiaki Kawahata, creator of a particularly famous origami Yoda.

Cool folks: Cece Bell, Charlie and Oscar, Raymond Loewy, George and Barbara Bell, the Hemphills, Madelyn Rosenberg, Steve Altis, Linda Acorn, Farida Dowler, Ken Leonard, the

Kidlitosphere, Will and Rhonda, Kids In The Valley Adventuring, Sean and the diabolo.ca community, Cindy Minnick, Paula Alston and Co., Lolly Rosemond, Mrs. Doughty, Mrs. Campbell, Caryn Wiseman, Susan Van Metre, Chad Beckerman, Melissa Arnst, Scott Auerbach, Jason Wells, the Great Wastoli, Sam Riddleburger, Carol Roeder, and the dude who made it all possible, Van Jahnke.

And with gratitude to Mr. Randall for lessons in computers, physics, and life.

ABOUT THE AUTHOR

Write this novel, Yoda told Tom Angleberger
he must. Long before he followed the advice
of Yoda, Tom applied for a job as a newspaper
artist but was mistakenly assigned a writing
position. Fifteen years later he is still at
it, currently as a columnist for the *Roanoke
Times* in Roanoke, Virginia. He lives in
Christianburg, Virginia, with his wife. Visit
him online at www.origamiyoda.com.

This book was designed by Melissa Arnst and art directed by Chad W. Beckerman. The main text is set in 10 point Lucida Sans Typewriter. The display typeface is ERASER. Tommy's comments are set in Kienan, and Harvey's comments are set in Good Dog. The hand lettering on the cover was done by Jason Rosenstock.

KEEP READING!
IF YOU LIKED THIS BOOK,
CHECK OUT THESE OTHER TITLES.

Attack of the Fluffy Bunnies
By Andrea Beaty
978-0-8109-8416-5
$12.95 HARDCOVER

NERDS
Book One: National Espionage, Rescue, and Defense Society
By Michael Buckley
978-0-8109-4324-7
$14.95 HARDCOVER

NERDS
Book Two: M is for Mama's Boy
By Michael Buckley
978-0-8109-8986-3
$14.95 HARDCOVER

KEEP READING!

IF YOU LIKED THIS BOOK, CHECK OUT THESE OTHER TITLES.

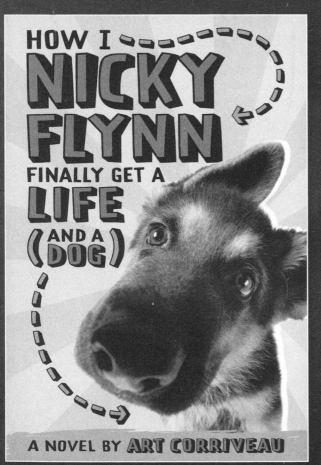

How I, Nicky Flynn, Finally Get a Life (and a Dog)
By Art Corriveau
978-0-8109-8298-7
$16.95 HARDCOVER